MEDINA HILL

TRILBY KENT

TUNDRA BOOKS

Published in Canada by Tundra Books,
75 Sherbourne Street, Toronto, Ontario M5A 2P9

Published in the United States by Tundra Books of Northern New York,
P.O. Box 1030, Plattsburgh, New York 12901

Library of Congress Control Number: 2008909727

Library and Archives Canada Cataloguing in Publication
Kent, Trilby
Medina Hill / Trilby Kent.
ISBN 978-0-88776-888-0
I. Title.

PS8571.E643M43 2009   jC813'.54   C2008-906638-3

We acknowledge the financial support of the Government of Canada
through the Book Publishing Industry Development Program (BPIDP) and
that of the Government of Ontario through the Ontario Media
Development Corporation's Ontario Book Initiative. We further acknowledge the support of the Canada Council for the Arts and the Ontario Arts
Council for our publishing program.

ONTARIO ARTS COUNCIL
CONSEIL DES ARTS DE L'ONTARIO

Design: Kelly Hill

Printed and bound in Canada

This book is printed on acid-free paper that is 100% recycled,
ancient-forest friendly (40% post-consumer recycled).

1   2   3   4   5   6   14   13   12   11   10   09

To Mum and Dad,
who taught me that life is an adventure,
and to Daniel,
for sharing that adventure with me.

"All men dream, but not equally. Those who dream by night in the dusty recesses of their minds wake in the day to find that it was vanity: but the dreamers of the day are dangerous men, for they may act their dream with open eyes, to make it possible. This I did."

T. E. LAWRENCE, *The Seven Pillars of Wisdom*
Suppressed introductory chapter,
first published 1939

ONE

This story began long before I wandered into it.

The story's not entirely mine, after all: Sancha would tell things her way. Then again, if you were very brave and tried to ask the Reverend Cleary – who's been dead for ages now – you'd get another version altogether. According to him, I might only make it in by one toe, like a bandit who jumps onto a moving train just in time to escape the sheriff on his tail.

I could begin with the day an ancient burial ground was discovered on the banks of the Euphrates back in 1913, but like I said, the story began without me. For one thing, I hadn't been born when that happened.

Being born was just about the only exciting thing to happen for the first eleven years of my life. When I was eight, I lost a tiny corner of one tooth – it's called a canine – after Ronald Kerring thumped me on the way home from school. When I was nine, I thumped him back. And when I was ten, Dad took me to see *King Kong* in Leicester Square.

Until the summer of 1935, that's about as thrilling as it got. It feels a bit silly saying it now, but for the longest time I didn't know that there were people who could speak with the dead, or that you could sum up a person's life by the number of pork pies he had stored away in an ice box. I didn't know that getting kicked by a Gypsy girl hurts a lot more if she's got a wooden leg. Or that on a narrow strip of the Cornish coast, you might discover a pocket of the Arabian Desert. These were all things I had yet to learn.

These were all things that I learned, in one way or another, from a man called Lawrence.

But first you need to know how it was that I forgot how to speak.

It was a long division question that did it. The air in our classroom was thick with chalk dust as Miss Hopkins peered at me through spectacles that had slid down to the bulge in her nose.

"I'm waiting, Dominic," she repeated.

Sixty-three. Easy.

"Sixty-three, stupid," hissed Bruno behind me.

I know, I know—

He had some nerve, the duffer. Bruno was good at

making owl noises and getting teased by girls: that was about the extent of his talents.

"We're still waiting, Dominic." Mrs. Hopkins' tone had sharpened.

Some of the girls began to twitter. Bruno sighed too loudly. Even my best friend, Frankie, rolled his eyes.

"Awright, old boy?"

"Quiet, Frankie!" snapped Mrs. Hopkins.

I studied the letters that someone had scratched into the wooden desk with a compass; the inkwell caked with black crust. No sound came.

Sixty-three. Sss-icks-tee-thhh-reee. The harder I concentrated on forming those simple noises, the less they seemed to make sense. I stuttered something incoherent, I felt myself grow hot, I raged inwardly as the know-it-alls continued to stare. Mrs. Hopkins grew exasperated; she saw that I'd written in my jotter and assumed that I was just messing about. I got a cuff on the head and was told not to play the fool.

"One hundred lines by tomorrow, Dominic: *I will not be obstinate.*"

Don't ask me how it happened. Dad always said I was a walking gob as a little kid. I used to talk rubbish with my mates all the time, egging them on, cutting them down, acting tough and clever even when I knew that they knew I was just a baby who still begged Mum to make her special gingerbread at Christmas.

1935 had been a bad year. Only a few weeks after Mum started coughing blood, Dad lost his job on the

import desk at Millwall Dock. It was the only job he'd
ever had. He'd gone to fight in the Great War when he
was seventeen, and when he returned the only thing
he could do was stamp duties and open and shut filing
cabinets. Losing the job at Millwall Dock while being
so worried about Mum must have felt like being torn in
two after getting trampled by an elephant; two kinds of
pain, each as bad as the other.

Things went from rotten to worse. When I started
Year Six, kids I hadn't known before began to take over
our little group, rewriting the unwritten social code,
drawing in my old mates like safety pins to a magnet.
On really bad days, I'd pretend not to hear when someone spoke to me, hoping that my silence made me look
impressive rather than awkward.

When Miss Hopkins first mentioned this to Mum,
neither of my parents believed her.

"Dominic never stops gabbing at home," they'd
insisted. "He's always on at his sister, or begging us for
cinema money – just like any boy. Worse, even."

And I was. Just not *Out There*: at school, or on the
street, or at the laundrette where Mum found work while
Dad waited for a new job. It wasn't that I couldn't think
of things to say; I just couldn't say them. And not being
able to speak made my world a very small place indeed.

I'd lived in Mudchute all my life. That's a real part of
London, even though people think it's a funny name:
they called it that because of the mud channels used to
construct the docks. Growing up in the East End, there

wasn't a lot going for a kid who didn't talk. If you were a boy, you had to whip up a reputation through your chat then nail it home with a few victories in the odd back-alley brawl. I wasn't a tough kid. You needed a name like Mick to be tough; you needed greasy black hair and hand-me-down clothes. I tried to get people to call me Dom, but that didn't catch on. My hair was yellow and a little too curly, and my eyelashes were so long that I'd once heard Mrs. Schlink down the road describe them as "girlish." Mum always made sure that my sweaters were properly darned and my socks matched. The fact that I couldn't defend myself with words made me a sitting duck.

The only people I could speak to were Mum, Dad, and my sister, Marlo. But Mum was spending more and more time resting. When I tried to make her feel better by telling her about my day, Dad would warn me not to be so demanding and to give her some peace.

"Tell me anyway, angel."

Mum would look at me upside down, not moving her head. She found it difficult even to crane her neck just the teensiest bit. She struggled to keep her eyes open.

"Lad, your mum needs some rest."

"But she just said – "

Mum would place a cool hand on mine, silencing me. She looked very young then – not in a lovely way, but small. Weak. It's not nice seeing your mum look so vulnerable.

"Maybe I'll sleep for a little while, angel. Then you can tell me what happened."

I would have liked to talk to Dad, to ask him questions about the war – like how many Germans he killed or what a mortar bomb sounds like or if he knew anyone who was gassed. But Dad didn't want to talk about those things, and I couldn't think of anything to ask about the import desk, so that didn't leave us with very much.

Then there was Marlo. To be honest, I liked her a lot more than I let on in front of my mates. There's always a fat kid who gets teased at school, and Marlo was it. She wasn't even properly fat; just chubby, really, with big round cheeks and a podgy little tummy and squoshy legs. Mum's friends always fussed over her, which didn't help. Her smile was a bit too toothy, and she cried a lot. At eight years, she was still stuck between the safety of being babied, and the humiliation of not growing up fast enough.

We were a right pair, Marlo and me.

It hadn't always been so difficult. When we were little kids, we'd have lots of fun on the channels: using the abandoned conveyors as slides, digging forts in the riverbank, playing at being pirates or white slaves, and pottering through the muddy overspill hunting for newts. But by the time I turned eleven, no one wanted to trade fag cards with me, and I was usually left out of games like Tippy-cat or Knock-down Ginger. If I was really unlucky, I'd end up in the center of a circle of kids waiting to see me get beaten up or stuck on the hot-water pipes behind the old pumping station.

It was usually Ronald Kerring's gang that did this. Ronald was two years older than me, and he took a special pride in inspecting the burn marks that the pipes left on his victims' legs. Every week, he'd get his posse to pick a random kid so that he could check to see that the scars were still there. If he was satisfied with the branding, he'd grin and pat the lad on the back as if they were old chums. Whenever it was my turn to be inspected, Marlo would try to intervene. This never helped. Surprisingly, getting ratted on by the tubby kid didn't do much to charm the bullies.

Now listen: I'm not looking for sympathy. But this is how things were before I knew anything exciting would happen; before Lawrence and Sancha and the Reverend Cleary.

This is how it was before a visit from Uncle Roo changed everything.

TWO

The day he came, Marlo was on the stairs reading about oxtail casserole. Around the same time that I lost my voice, my sister had gone a little funny in her own way. Despite appearances, she didn't stuff her face for comfort. But when she was off school with whooping cough, Marlo had discovered Mum's only cookbook. And there was something in there that filled her up and satisfied her in a way that a few friends might have done, if she'd had them.

"Why don't you ever make us quail's eggs?" she'd asked Mum one evening, greedily eyeing the illustrations between neat columns of instructions.

Mum had smiled weakly, stirring a watery broth on the hob. I'd seen her almost toss out the book before. Having never used any of the fancy recipes, perhaps it made her feel a little guilty. Marrow jelly, mushy peas, bread and dripping, pork belly sold off cheap on Saturday nights – that's the sort of thing we got most evenings. And we loved her cooking, really we did.

My sister wasn't complaining, mind. But *The New Art of Cooking* had opened another world for her. I guess it was an escape. There was a section called "Feasts from the Arabian Nights," and another one called "Medieval Meats, Meads, and Mushrooms." Marlo took to carrying it around with her the way a baby clings to her blanket.

"You don't even know how to boil water," I'd sneered at her, irritated by the fact that she seemed so content, safe in a world of Sunday roasts and jelly trifles. "What's the point of reading a book for housewives?"

Marlo had gazed up at me with those dumb, gray eyes and replied, "You wouldn't understand."

She had a point. I still don't know if she memorized the recipes or just looked at the pictures.

That day, as she hunched over the recipe for oxtail casserole, I'd been perched on the landing – flicking rubber bands in her hair, winding her up to see if she'd cry – when a funny tapping noise started on the front window. I noticed it in time to see a gray blur flapping against the glass. Then it vanished.

"It's the Baron!"

In an instant, Marlo forgot about her recipes and lurched for the door.

Uncle Roo was standing on our crumbling front step, hands on hips, neck arched, squinting into the sun.

"Get down from there, you pesky creature," he muttered. "Honestly! I let you out of your basket for one moment . . ."

We scrambled outside to peer up at the eaves trough with him. Baron Sigwalt — at twenty-two, the oldest surviving carrier pigeon of the war — was busily pecking at some leaves protruding from a rusty drainpipe. The bird swivelled his smooth gray head to consider us, three gormless humans. He blinked. We blinked.

"I said, get down from there! Or I'll see you served up in a pie before you can say – "

"Hullo, Uncle Roo!"

Pretending to be surprised, our uncle reeled on one foot.

"Children!" He swung Marlo into the air and ruffled my hair. Uncle Roo was very thin and very tall, with a neat gray mustache and crinkly eyes. He addressed us as if we were grown-ups, with the refinement of a distinguished gent. "My apologies for the Baron's ghastly manners. It's the city. He's overexcited. He thinks the other pigeons are taking the mick. Can't comprehend their infernal Cockney twang . . ."

"Rupert!"

Mum had appeared in the doorway, white arms outstretched. Uncle Roo swept her into a great bear hug.

"Such a commotion! It could only mean one thing." Dad emerged from the dim hallway with a tired smile.

"Good man, good man!" Uncle Roo pumped Dad's hand. "Has your wife got some water on? I'd love a cuppa, now that you mention it."

We piled inside. For the first time in ages, the house was full of life.

Uncle Roo was Mum's elder brother. He'd been a *C.O.* in the Great War, a "conscientious objector," which meant that he'd refused to fight. He didn't believe in armies and killing, and he didn't see why England had any business getting involved in European squabbles. So, he was called up in front of a group of military men who had to decide if he'd be forced to join the army or put in prison or set to work in some way that would still help the war effort. In the end, he was allowed to remain at home, but on the condition that he take a farm in Cornwall and produce food for the soldiers many miles away – raising bees for their honey and wax, and growing sugar beet and maize. The other thing that Uncle Roo got to do was train pigeons to carry messages to the front lines. According to him, one of his birds was awarded the Victoria Cross for making it all the way to France and back.

After the war, Uncle Roo sold most of the pigeons, but he continued to produce prizewinning honey at Cornish market fairs. His wife – Auntie Sylv to Marlo and me – stopped being a schoolteacher and started to paint. Mum and Dad said it was a wonder that they managed to survive like that, but then Mum and Dad had never approved much of Uncle Roo being a C.O.

"All the scholarships in the world can't excuse cowardice," Dad once said. When Mum told him it wasn't cowardice that kept Uncle Roo from fighting, but years of careful thought, Dad had only replied, "The rest of us didn't have time for careful thought in the trenches. We were too bloody busy defending king and country, trying not to get killed."

He may have been right, but I didn't hold it against my uncle. The war was long over, and although some people were talking about another one starting up, we had worse things to worry about.

"So how are you, Dominic my boy?" asked Uncle Roo, sinking into a chair. "What god-awful music are you lads listening to nowadays?"

"Jelly Roll Morton's all right . . . and Fats Waller," I offered, suddenly shy. I'd not seen Uncle Roo since I'd forgotten how to talk to people who weren't family. For all I knew, he thought I was still a normal boy.

"What kind of names are those?"

"Don't you like jazz, Uncle Roo?"

"American codswallop!" My uncle waved a dismissive hand, almost knocking over his teacup. "Why can't you people listen to proper music?" Part of him was being serious; but there was a twinkle in his eye.

"More tea, Uncle Roo?" offered Marlo.

"Thank you, darling girl. And what is that you're reading?"

Marlo beamed. "Recipes, Uncle Roo. Oxtail casserole."

"*Ugh.*"

"And cowslip pudding. Fruit cake with brandy cream. Strawberry meringues . . ."

"Now you're speaking my language!"

Marlo's grin widened, exposing the gap where she'd recently lost a front tooth. It made a soft whistling noise every time she said *s*.

"And gooseberry tansy. Apple Charlotte. Here's a lemon posset. Fruit syllabub, see? Queen's Pudding, too. And eggs with marigolds and sorrel and moules – "

"What are you doing in London, Uncle Roo?"

For a split second, the room felt very still. Outside, Baron Sigwalt continued to rattle at the drainpipe.

"It's funny you should ask that, my dear boy."

Mum opened her mouth to speak, thought better of it, and folded her hands in her lap. Dad glanced at Uncle Roo, then looked to me.

"Your uncle has come to us with an exciting proposal."

"Ooh!" Marlo's round face crumpled into a giant grin. "Tell, tell!"

I peered at Mum. There was something in her silence that didn't feel right. She wasn't looking at either of us. Uncle Roo shifted in his chair.

"Well, I'd not expected you to ask that quite so soon." He eyed Marlo, a smile tugging at the corners of his mouth. "But now that you have, I suppose I'd better come clean."

Once again, the room was still.

"I've come to invite you to spend the summer with us. In Cornwall."

"Cor! Can we, Dad?"

"Your mother and I have already discussed it. We've agreed that you two should go."

"But – you and Mum won't come?" Marlo's excitement immediately gave way to apprehension. She folded her arms. "Mum has to come, too."

My father inhaled slowly. Mum beckoned Marlo to her.

"You know Mummy's not well," she explained. "The doctors have said it would be good for me to go into hospital for a little while, to get my strength back. What with Dad starting a new job soon, there won't be anyone at home to look after you. Besides, you and Dominic could both do with the fresh air."

"I don't want to go without Mum!" wailed Marlo.

"Stay here, then," I snapped. It felt spiteful, but I couldn't stand the kid spoiling my chance to see the country. I'd never been outside of London.

"Don't speak to your sister like that," interrupted my father. He fixed me with a hard look. "This is as much about getting you sorted out, young man. Don't forget there'll be other people there with you. We want you to shake out of this no talking business by the time you're back at school, understood?"

"Stephen, that's not fair." Mum turned to Uncle Roo. "Dominic's not being stubborn, it's just anxiety. He's perfectly fine with us; he only clams up in front of strangers – "

"He goes mute," said Dad.

"He doesn't choose to, though. He can't help it."

I felt a lump catch in my throat. So that's what this was all about.

"What do you mean, 'other people'?" I whispered.

I could tell that Uncle Roo was feeling unnerved by the rise in tension. He swallowed nervously.

"Auntie Sylv and I have started up a co-operative, Dominic. A sort of artists' colony for people who want to write or paint or compose music away from the hustle and bustle of modern life. But you needn't worry. There are only three of them at the moment, and they're all lovely. They're very keen to meet you both."

He was trying; I couldn't blame him for that. But I glared at Dad through narrowed eyes.

"You're trying to get rid of us."

"Darling, that's not true!" Mum's expression was strained, and I immediately regretted my words.

"It's a chance for us all," said Dad, in a low voice that made it clear the discussion was closed.

As Marlo whimpered into Mum's apron, Baron Sigwalt fluttered to the window ledge outside. With a bossy *Croo-croo!* he puffed up his breast feathers and blinked impatiently. *Ready to go,* he seemed to say.

THREE

Grown-up conspiracies were nothing new to us.

There'd been a conspiracy before, between Mum and Dad and the doctors. Mum's lungs had always been weak, but that winter she'd started to cough a lot more, mainly after meals, or if she'd been working really hard scrubbing floors at the houses in Greenwich. The doctors told her that the damp in our house was making it hard for her to breathe, but what were we to do, living near the river and with a landlord who demanded five pounds we didn't have before he'd fix the leaking pipes?

Dad didn't talk about Mum's illness, other than to bark halfheartedly at us when we pestered her for attention. Sometimes Mrs. Schlink from down the road would come to help tidy the house and cook for me and Marlo. Even though it was just one or two days a week, it seemed that she was always in our kitchen, smoking her smelly cigars, fussing and puffing and putting things away in places where they didn't belong. I hated the way she managed our cups and saucers as if they were hers, the way she set the table with the knives and forks side by side. Mrs. Schlink didn't like children, so there was no getting any sense out of her. The doctors avoided me and Marlo. No one gave Mum's illness a name, like mumps or measles or jungle fever, and not having a name meant we couldn't understand it. At least jungle fever would have given us something to talk about.

Then there was Dad. Mum once told me that Dad had come back from the war a broken man. But he wasn't a cripple like Steve Reid's dad, or a mumbling loony like Mr. Cranmer down the road. I couldn't see any scars or splints or dressings. There was something fishy about that, too.

Of course, to the grown-ups it wasn't a conspiracy. In the days leading up to Uncle Roo's visit, they must have told themselves that we'd be chuffed to bits to go to Cornwall all on our own. When Mum received the tippity-tapped reply from Auntie Sylv, rat-a-tapped in from a telegraph office half a world away, she must have been really pleased with herself. After all, planning to send me and Marlo to the countryside was "doing what's best for the children." I suppose when they looked around our neighborhood, they only saw dreary roads divided up by patches of black earth, houses tee-tering beneath crooked, soot-stained chimneys, weed-strewn gardens, dripping archways, and grim wharves like teeth gnawing the river. They probably thought it wasn't much of a place for children, especially when we could be living by the sea with miles of fields all around and friendly towns where you know everyone's name and all the houses have front gardens full of flowers. They may have had a point. But they could have asked me first.

"My stomach hurts," mumbled Marlo, slumping in her seat. She hugged *The New Art of Cooking* to her chest, peering over the cover with a sulky scowl. We'd been waiting on the train an hour already, her and me and Uncle Roo, wedged in between suitcases and coats. Why Mum had insisted on sending us off with two duffels in July, I'll never know.

"Why don't we get up and stretch our legs?" suggested Uncle Roo. "The train's going to be delayed another half hour – I heard the porters say so. Perhaps something's wrong in the engine cab."

"I can't move," moped Marlo, sinking even lower behind her cookbook. "My *stomach*."

Uncle Roo caught my eye, feigning concern with a conspiratorial twinkle.

"Perhaps she's hungry? Nothing a ginger beer and toffee apple wouldn't remedy, I'm sure."

Marlo was trying valiantly to look unimpressed. I nodded, sharing in the joke.

"What do you say, Dominic?"

I continued to nod, skirting Uncle Roo's gaze by watching two ladies struggle to heave an overstuffed suitcase on to the train. *Don't wait for me to say something.*

*You know I can't – not here, with all these people looking at us
like we're a couple of charity cases. I can't.*

"He doesn't say much, Uncle Roo. Not in front of
strangers."

I shot Marlo an icy glare and thumped her on the arm.
"Ow!"

"Come on, Dominic, let's see to those ginger beers,
hm? Marlo, you keep an eye on the Baron."

It didn't take us long to find a teashop outside
Waterloo station. Uncle Roo bought me a bag of barley
twists and ginger beer and a packet of chocolate biscuits for us to share later. It was all I could do to keep
myself from ripping the waxy brown paper bags open
right then and there. The toffee tin at home had been
empty for a very long time. There was a picture of the
young princesses on the lid, and Dad used to joke that
this meant we could say we had royalty round for tea.
The pictures showed them playing in the garden, or
posing in all their finery before Buckingham Palace.
Dad used to line the tins out along the kitchen table and
ask if Elizabeth would mind passing the chocolate
digestives, and if little Margaret, with her mop of
golden hair, wouldn't like some warm milk to go with
her violet creams.

We had stopped playing this game when Dad lost
his job. Now, King George and Queen Mary remained
with their granddaughters high up on the highest shelf,
behind the sacks of flour and sugar that Mother didn't
use because she no longer had the heart for baking.

"Shall we take a wander?" asked Uncle Roo, as I sucked ravenously on one of the barley twists. "The last time I was here, there was a splendid bookshop just around the corner."

I groaned inwardly. We had enough books shoved at us in school. Still, a few minutes would be a fair trade-off for all those sweets.

The floorboards creaked as we entered Sandhalls, wending our way between teetering stacks of books piled almost to the ceiling. We had entered a world of brown: oak brown, mahogany brown, liver brown. Copper railings lined shelves displaying maroon bindings and russet spines. I wondered how many sepia pages were contained in that single shop; how many gold tassels and tan labels. It smelled of binding glue and printing ink, floor polish and old woolly jumpers. I watched as a young woman in a cloche hat carefully opened a thick leather volume, her slender fingers gently feeling the pages. When she closed the book, fine wisps of dust shot out through a narrow shaft of sunlight like so many tiny sprites.

Dad would have frowned at the collegiate mezzanine and elegant skylights, the fabric wallpaper printed with blue and green birds. He would have dismissed it all as far too posh for the likes of us. Mum would have worried that the sighing oak gallery might topple from above and crush unwary customers. My parents weren't exactly book lovers. We owned a weathered copy of Grimms' fairy tales, but Mum had glued most of the pages together when I was little and easily frightened. They wouldn't have known where to begin in Sandhalls. But Uncle Roo plunged headlong into a back room like a puppy let off its lead for the first time, leaving me to fend for myself.

There were one or two other people browsing the shelves, and an elderly man perched like a vulture on a high stool behind the counter. What was I supposed to do? Follow Uncle Roo into the secondhand stacks? I'd look a proper tagalong. Ask the shopkeeper for a book? I couldn't think of any titles. This wasn't the kind of shop that sold comics. I felt a wash of irritation prickle at my skin. I was scared. Scared and annoyed at being plucked out of a familiar world and dumped in this strange one. I wanted to go home.

"What have you found, then?"

Uncle Roo reappeared unexpectedly, clutching two tattered volumes to his chest.

People sometimes asked me if I was tongue-tied. But when you can't speak, it's not because of anything wrong with your tongue. It's your throat that's the problem; as if it's stuffed full of cotton wool. Right then, it felt as if it was swelling like a balloon as I tried to muster a casual reply.

"Nothing much," I whispered hoarsely, straining to complete the sentence. With every word, I felt the shopkeeper's gaze on my back, like a teasing finger running up and down my spine. How long had I been standing there? I avoided Uncle Roo's eager gaze.

"Nothing much?" His tone was baffled. "Out of all this, nothing much?"

I scanned the shelves desperately, terrified of disappointing him. I grabbed a book at random; or maybe not quite at random. Its green spine was out of place in the wash of brown. "This." I mouthed the word soundlessly.

"Ah, and what have we here?" Uncle Roo peered down his nose at the front cover, holding the book at arm's length as he squinted to make out the title. "*Incredible Adventures for Boys: Colonel Lawrence and the Revolt in the Desert.*" He declaimed it as if it were a line from Shakespeare.

I shifted nervously, praying for approval.

"An interesting choice, Dominic."

Interesting?

He looked back at me and thrust the book into my hands.

"It's yours, then. Something for the journey, hm?"

I couldn't say no. Never mind that I wasn't remotely interested in spending a whole day on the train reading a book; never mind that I'd never heard of Colonel Lawrence; never mind that I didn't care. I smiled weakly.

Gosh – thanks, Uncle Roo.

He strode up to the counter and placed the book, along with the two he was carrying, before the shopkeeper.

"My nephew is an avid reader," he declared, proudly. The shopkeeper stared at me sourly. I shoved my hands deep in my pockets.

"Lawrence: the uncrowned king of the Arabs. Did you know that the first draft of his memoirs was lost after the war?" Uncle Roo rambled on cheerily as if he and the shopkeeper were old friends. "It was stolen at a railway station. He had to rewrite the whole thing from scratch. No one knows what happened to the original."

The shopkeeper nodded slowly. "Sixpence apiece," he muttered.

"Larger than life," continued Uncle Roo, painstakingly sorting the change from his wallet. "He was one of the few heroes of that shameful mess of a war. Scarce things, these days – heroes. England could use more men like him in times such as these. A latter-day Arthur."

"Silly way to die," grunted the shopkeeper. I looked up at Uncle Roo.

"A motorcycle accident near his home a few months ago," he explained to me, in a low voice. "Lawrence swerved to avoid a couple of boys on bicycles. They survived, but he–"

"Would you like those in a bag, sir?" interrupted the shopkeeper.

I shook my head vigorously.

"What's that? Oh, no – no, not to worry. Thank you." Uncle Roo paid for the books and passed them to me as the till clinked shut.

We made it back just as the train had started to belch billows of black smoke, each gust punctuated by a piercing whistle. In his wicker basket, Baron Sigwalt was flapping perturbedly, ignoring Marlo's attempts to calm him. She glared at us accusingly.

"Where have you been? The Baron's upset."

"He always gets antsy before a journey," replied Uncle Roo. "It's normal."

"What's that?" Marlo pointed at the green book resting in my lap.

I shrugged, fingering the embossed gold letters on the hard cloth cover. Beneath the title was a picture of a man in an Arabian headpiece – a bit like the dishcloth I'd worn at the school Nativity play, when I'd been one of the Three Wise Men. He didn't look like a Wise Man from the East, but he looked wise enough. A wise version of the Irish grocer on the corner of Mellish Street.

I shoved the book into my bag and tried not to think of home.

FOUR

t was a long journey, much longer than I'd expected. By the time the train pulled into Penzance railway station, we might as well have arrived in Australia. Marlo had spent most of the time dozing restlessly, cramming her head into the crook of my elbow, round white knees pushed up against the window as we rumbled alongside the swerving coast. When I finally dislodged myself, one side of her face was pink and dimpled where she had pressed against my arm. Her hair clips had slid askew, and her auburn curls were dishevelled.

"Where are we?" she asked groggily, straightening her frock.

"Almost there now," whispered Uncle Roo. "Look." He pointed to a craggy point rising from the water at the curve in the coast, fringed with palm trees. "St Michael's

Mount. You can walk to it when the tide's low. And
that's Marazion."

A lot of the Cornish place names I'd heard sounded
very un-English – almost biblical. Marazion was one
of them. Zelah was another.

Liskeard. Men Scryfa. Polzeath. Tintagel. Mevagissey.
Morvah. Lelant.

Zennor.

"It's seven miles from here," said Uncle Roo, bal-
ancing the Baron's cage on his lap as he gathered the
bags. "Otto said that he'd meet us with the car. It's a
lovely drive to the north coast."

My sister reached for her recipe book. "Will there be
dinner?"

"Is the pope Catholic? Of course!" Uncle Roo
tweaked Marlo's nose, making her giggle. "The Reverend
Cleary will be a little late, but Birdie should be back
from her séance in plenty of time. Your Auntie Sylv will
feed us so much that we'll have to be rolled into bed!"

My sister brightened at the news. I had already gone
cold at the thought of meeting the other three – Otto
and Birdie, and the Reverend Cleary. Whoever they
were, they'd expect me to talk.

"Come on, Dominic!"

There was no mistaking Otto. He was leaning against
an electric blue MG with gleaming silver headlights as
large as mixing bowls, one foot propped against a
chrome hubcap, nonchalantly wiping down the hood.
The canvas roof had been rolled back, revealing plush

leather seats. As soon as he caught sight of us trudging wearily from the station, he waved his yellow handkerchief with a dramatic flourish.

"Greetings, friends!"

Otto was easily two feet shorter than Uncle Roo, about ten years younger, and a good deal fatter. His bald head shone almost as brightly as the headlights, and his rosy cheeks were the size of apples. He wore a three-piece suit, like a pantomime character: a bright canary waistcoat to match his kerchief, and a checkered blue and green jacket to complement the car. His trousers reached almost to his armpits, snug around a belly that trembled like jelly in a mold.

"Let me, please!" Beaming, he grabbed our briefcases with fingers thick as sausages before anyone could think to respond. I breathed a sigh of relief that he didn't seem to expect a reply from me, at least. "Not much space, I'm afraid," he explained, yanking a leather strap across the back seat to secure the luggage. He shot me a side-long glance. "The little one might have to ride on top."

As we sped through Cornwall's narrow country lanes, hemmed in by dense hedges and veering as madly as if we were on a Snakes and Ladders board, I felt a rush of liberation. The trees up ahead gleamed golden against a steel-blue sky. It was my favorite kind of sky: the kind where the sun is behind you and the clouds are ahead of you, but the sun illuminates the leaves in the trees like hundreds of fluttering electric lights. The black clouds made them seem brighter.

Otto drove fearlessly – recklessly, Mum might have said – accelerating at junctions, thrusting his full weight into every turn, bouncing merrily in his seat with yelps of glee as we flew over potholes and sandy patches.

"Glorious, isn't she?" he shouted. "Pure speed!"

Uncle Roo twisted himself around to face us. "Otto's hobby," he explained. "When he's not writing those blasted potboilers, that is."

"Don't believe a thing he tells you!" shouted Otto. He glanced over his shoulder at Marlo. "All right, there, kiddo?"

Marlo nodded emphatically, clutching at her seat with white knuckles.

"We're not actually in Zennor," said Uncle Roo. "Medina Hill is a short distance from the town. You'll be able to see the sea."

"Sublime!" exclaimed Otto, his shiny bald dome wagging with exuberance. "Magnificent! Splendid!"

We were now following a narrow strip of road over a rugged moor, a wild landscape that was worlds away from the quaint countryside I'd imagined. Slate and granite boulders were scattered in desolate clusters across the windswept fields, their brooding forms brushed by yellow grass that seemed to bow in hushed reverence as we flashed by.

Ahead of us, a few houses clung to the hillside over-looking the sea. At every bend, it was just possible to spot foaming white waves, lashing at the rocky coves, and seabirds circling the cliffs. Some distance from the houses, a cluster of painted wagons formed a jagged circle near a copse of bent trees.

"What are those?" asked Marlo.

"The Romany!"

"Who?"

"Traveling folk," explained Uncle Roo, with a nod. "They come every summer to pick fruit and trade horses, and they leave as soon as the leaves begin to turn. A few are metal workers, much more skilled than your average village smithy. They always follow the same route. For wanderers, they're pretty regular."

"Cornwall has been good to them!" confirmed Otto.

"People do complain, though. They let their children run riot, and they play music late into the night. Plenty of local farmers would like to take control of that land, from the foot of Medina Hill all the way to Trewhalley Wood. It runs right the way up to Tinner's Path."

I wanted to ask Otto to take a detour, to drive us past the wagons so that I could see these mysterious Travelers. I wanted to ask what kind of music they played, how their children were any different from me or Marlo. I wanted to shout hello as the car screamed by.

But of course, I couldn't.

We were approaching the mightiest of the green cliffs. A steep slope wound up the side, tailing off around a bend.

"This is the fun bit!"

With a screech, the vehicle spun around so that it looked as though Otto might send us to a watery grave.

Instead, he plunged the car into reverse, straight up the curved drive, barely pausing to glance behind him as branches and leaves brushed our cheeks. It was a good minute before we ground to a halt, suspended on a level patch with the nose of the car pointing directly down the drive. I was too terrified to look back lest the slightest movement send us hurtling down the rocky cliffside. It was already getting dark and I would have to wait until morning to see the house clearly; all I could make out through the dusky shadows was that it was built of yellow stone.

Grinning broadly, Otto paused to mop his brow with the yellow kerchief.

"Home at last! Pile out, children – it's time to meet the family."

FIVE

The person introduced to us as Birdie looked as if she should have been telling fortunes outside one of the Gypsy wagons in the valley below. She wore a fuschia headscarf that trailed almost to the floor, and she had an American accent. I'd never met a real live American before.

"My parents thought that it would be a good idea to call me Eudora Bernadine," she drawled, with an ironic smile. "They should have been locked up for child cruelty. Everyone calls me Birdie."

The chunky metal bracelets stacked to her elbows jangled as she reached for the butter. Auntie Sylv smiled gently at me as I tried not to stare. Birdie's cheeks were flushed with heavy blotches of blush, blue eyeliner had been applied with a shaky hand, and her fingers were smudged with black charcoal.

"Birdie is a clairvoyant," explained Auntie Sylv.

The kitchen was almost as big as our house. Iron molds were hung about the lime-washed walls, and a fire crackled heartily in an enormous tumbledown stone fireplace. The six of us were seated in brightly painted chairs around a table with clawed feet. Before us were steaming dishes of roast chicken, fried dumplings, tomato and cucumber salad, turnips, parsnips and beets, applesauce, leek pie, smoked mackerel, potted cheese, fresh cornbread, and grilled limpets.

I'd never seen a limpet in my life, and I was none too sure about eating one. But using my fork to chase its shiny black shell around my plate was a wonderful way to avoid catching Birdie's eye. So far, no one had challenged me to speak.

"What's a clairvoyant?" asked Marlo. She swung her legs merrily as Auntie Sylv rolled three stewed beets onto her plate.

"It means that she speaks to people on the other side."

"The other side of what?"

There was an awkward silence as Marlo waited for an answer. Birdie sighed, and fixed my little sister with a wide stare.

"Do you know the greatest lie ever told, sweet-heart?" she asked patiently, blue eyes protruding and expressive. As she leaned in toward Marlo, I noticed that her frazzled red hair was peppery gray at the roots.

"No."

"*Death*. Death is the greatest lie ever told."

For a moment, all color drained from Marlo's face, turning her round cheeks ashen. The turnip on her fork froze on its way to her mouth.

"What do you mean?" she whispered.

Otto coughed loudly, busily stuffing a napkin into his collar.

"What she means, my dear, is that life doesn't end when we die. Our friend here *claims* to be able to call up the dead – "

"I don't call up *anyone*," interrupted Birdie, straightening herself. "If anything, they call *me*."

Otto snorted. "Make mine a drumstick, will you, Sylv?"

"The thing is," continued Birdie, warming to the conversation, "where I come from, *spiritualism* is getting a bad name. Too many fraudsters are using it to make a quick buck. They use all the old tricks – tapping on tables, speaking in tongues, making objects move on their own – to create a show for people. Then they get busted. And the rest of us, we take the rap."

"So you came all the way to England, Miss Birdie?" asked Marlo.

"That's right, sweetie. You folks still have a spiritual world. Not like the one I come from, full of gimmicks and loudmouth preachers. I hate to sound cynical, but the English lost a lot more men in the Great War. I've seen what happens to families when the news comes that their boy has died in some distant bloodbath. I was still a girl when my sister's fiancé copped it in a collapsed trench." She sighed. "The wounds cut deep, you know? It's been over fifteen years, and still there are people desperate to speak to their loved ones. Brothers, husbands, fathers, sons. Very sad it is, too."

Otto snorted again, flapping one hand in the air as if to order a new subject from an imaginary waiter. "Sylv, you've outdone yourself again," he sighed. His chair creaked wearily as he loosened his belt.

"You're too kind," laughed my aunt, modestly brushing aside a loose wisp of hair. She was wearing one of Uncle Roo's shirts with the sleeves rolled up, and I noticed how brown her arms had become. Her smooth cheeks glowed pink, and her clear eyes sparkled. I suppose that's what people mean when they say someone looks a picture of health. I tried to remember a time when Mum looked like that. I was still trying to remember when I felt a clumsy hand on my shoulder.

"So, young man," Otto was saying, "you must tell us the latest from London – the Big Thrill, the Black Smoke!"

It was the silence I dreaded most.

Marlo had seen it happen many times, so she was prepared for what came next. The tips of my ears would turn pink, a shocking shade of fear that spread slowly down my neck and across my face until I was bright red from the shoulders up. I'd wriggle in my seat, itchy with anxiety. My hands would go clammy, and I'd wipe them roughly on my shorts. I'd take a few deep breaths, each louder and more shallow than the last. Then I'd wait.

Uncle Roo and Auntie Sylv must have been warned. But Otto and Birdie clearly thought I was going to pass out.

"You all right, lad?" asked Otto, with a quizzical look. "Cat got your tongue?"

"Give him some air!" Birdie commanded. "You're stifling the poor thing."

Auntie Sylv rose to open the window.

"Dominic could use a little time to get settled in, that's all," explained Uncle Roo casually. "Why, the boy's just knackered from his journey – spent most of it gabbing away with the train driver, didn't you?"

I'd done no such thing, but he'd thrown me a lifeline I couldn't refuse. I forced myself to smile, nodding slowly at my plate.

Suddenly, Auntie Sylv began to wave at the window. "He's here!"

In a flash, all attention was diverted from me to the door. A gust of cool evening air swept through the kitchen, bringing with it a stooped, white-haired man. He coughed hoarsely as he heaved the door shut, leaning his walking stick against the wall with a clatter and removing his hat calmly and deliberately.

"Good evening to you all."

As he straightened, I noticed a white collar around his neck.

"Dominic, Marlo: the Reverend Cleary." Uncle Roo ushered the ancient gent to the empty seat at the head of the table, and Auntie Sylv began spooning barley soup into a bowl.

"Hello," chirped Marlo. She liked old people, possibly because they tended to fuss over her so much. She pointed to the soup. "Careful – it's hot."

The Reverend Cleary stared at her. After a moment, he smiled.

"Thank you, little girl. You may just have saved me a burnt tongue."

Marlo beamed.

"And – Dominic, is it?"

I nodded. *Please, not again.*

The Reverend seemed to consider me, pondering. His eyelashes were so white it was as if they'd been coated in frost. Then he shrugged, and looked deep into his bowl.

"Bloody awful Evensong tonight," he sighed.

I'd never heard a priest swear before.

"Did they play any of your stuff at the service, then?" asked Otto, cheerily.

"So they claimed!"

Otto grinned, elbowing me chummily. "Old Cleary here is something of a minor musical celebrity, you know."

The Reverend wheezed. It must have been the closest thing he could manage to a laugh. "If composing heart-felt songs of praise to be sung as dirges by a group of tone-deaf old biddies qualifies as celebrity – well, you know what you can do with celebrity."

Auntie Sylv shook her head, smiling. This was evidently a rant they'd heard before.

"You're too hard on them, Reverend."

"I am *not*," came the pointed reply. "The lot of them should be put out of their misery. Squawking like skinned cats, they were."

"Perhaps your compositions are too complex, Reverend," suggested Birdie. She rolled her eyes at me. "Perhaps the ladies of the parish need something a little more – simple."

"Simple? Was the Messiah *simple?* Bach's Mass in B Minor – was that *simple?*" The Reverend began to stir his soup furiously. "We should praise God with complexity that befits his majesty! Worshipping the Lord is no parlor trick, my dear."

"*Ugh!*" Birdie flung her arms wide, grimacing at us. "Do you see what I have to contend with here?"

"Contend!" exclaimed the Reverend. "You didn't have to contend with those damned Gypsy kids, hounding me for a handout all the way to the bottom of the hill. The sooner those people get booted off that land, the better!"

I wanted to stop him there, to ask about these "Gypsy kids." Did they beg? Were they so poor? Would they hound us, too?

But I remained silent.

"How are the drawings coming, Birdie?" asked Uncle Roo. He turned to me, talking very quickly to prevent any interruptions. "Birdie has created the most fantastic sketches, Dominic. She starts by going into a trance and lets her inner spirit guide the pencil–"

"Hogwash!" exclaimed the Reverend. "Trance! Inner spirit!"

Marlo began to giggle.

"'Do not trust every spirit,'" quoted the Reverend. "Gospel of John, chapter four, verse one!"

"I think it's time for dessert," piped Auntie Sylv. "Apple pie, anybody? There's cinnamon cake and burnt cream from yesterday, too – "

"If Jesus rose from the dead, why can't the rest of us?" wailed Birdie.

"Does anyone else hear what I'm hearing?"

Uncle Roo rose to collect the plates, stopping between me and Marlo to whisper, "Now might be a good time for me to show you your rooms, hm? You can have some cake later."

"Right, Uncle Roo," said Marlo with a twinkle. She leaned in towards me as we followed Uncle Roo to the stairs. "I think they're fun."

I shrugged, waiting to be out of earshot before replying.

"Fun? They're all mad. This is a right mess we've got ourselves into."

SIX

I struggled to get to sleep that night.

It wasn't that I was uncomfortable. I lay in a giant bed with a fat mattress and fresh, cool sheets. Auntie Sylv had left a jug full of wildflowers on the dressing table, and they filled the room with a gentle scent.

My room was in something like a loft; you had to climb a ship's ladder to get to it. It had a sloping ceiling with exposed beams, a window seat overlooking the garden, and a grinning papier mâché mask – probably something that my aunt had made – overlooking everything else. For the first time, Marlo was sleeping on her own, in a cozy room also with wide wooden floorboards and smooth walls painted yellow and blue. It was decorated with embroidered wall hangings and had several tin urns filled with forget-me-nots, corn-flowers, and poppies. Auntie Sylv had even left Marlo her own teddy – a lumpy little creature with bright button eyes and a sad smile – in the rocking chair by the bay window.

I'd never heard such silence. Outside, the world had been absorbed by a black night sky. No street lamps flickered through chinks in the curtains, no neighbors bickered noisily on the other side of the wall, no wireless scratched into tune, no doorbells shrilled, no babies squalled, no taps dripped. It should have been peaceful.

I anxiously flicked on the light at the bedside. It was reassuring to see that the room hadn't changed in the pitch darkness. My suitcase yawned at the foot of the bed.

With a sigh, I reached for the book crammed in among folded shirts, socks, and underwear. It felt solid and safe in my hands. I opened it, and began to read.

The story of the Arab Revolt is one of the greatest adventure tales in modern history, and at its center was a man named Thomas Edward Lawrence. Not only did this young Englishman help to win the largest war the world has ever seen, the Great War of 1914-1918, he also led a nation to freedom. Celebrated as a hero by his country, he insisted on giving whole credit to his comrades, the sheiks.

Yet, despite his fame, "Lawrence of Arabia" retreated from his legions of admirers after the war, retiring to a private life in the English countryside.

He seemed a funny kind of hero, wanting to hide away from the world. A bit like me – only I'd never done anything heroic. I kept reading.

> When he first tried to join up as a private to fight in the Great War, the medical officers simply laughed. The shy Oxford graduate before them was small and softly spoken, and looked to them more like a choirboy than a soldier. He was told to get back to school and wait for the next war.

Rotters. Something told me that the joke would be on them.

I carried on reading for a long time, losing myself in Lawrence's initial trip to Arabia, where he worked as an archaeologist and befriended the Arab boy Dahoum. Lawrence taught Dahoum to speak English, and Dahoum helped Lawrence with his Arabic. Working together at Carchemish, they unearthed mysterious stone stelae inscribed with strange hieroglyphs and at nearby Deve Huyuk, a small village on the Euphrates River, they discovered a military cemetery brimming with ancient Persian weapons, jewelry, and bronze. Lawrence later said that this had been the happiest time of his life.

After many pages, I was shaken from the story by a tentative knock at the door.

"Who's there?" I asked, unnerved by the sound of my own voice as it cut through the silence.

Marlo poked her head around the corner.

"It's me," she whispered. "I can't sleep."

"Come on, then," I said, making room for her on the bed. She clambered up, and eyed the green book.

"Is it any good?" she asked.

"All right."

"What's it about?"

I sighed. She always did this.

"It's about a bloke who was working as an archaeologist in Arabia when the war broke out. The Germans convinced the Turks to let them build a railroad from Berlin to Baghdad, right through Arab land. The English were none too pleased, so they got this fellow Lawrence onside to boot out the Turks."

"Why him?"

"Because he knew the camel routes, and how to survive in the desert, and he spoke Arabic. The Arabs liked him, too."

"Read me a bit."

"Marlo – "

"*Please?*"

I rolled my eyes.

The Arabian Desert is larger than Great Britain,
France, Spain, and Holland put together.

I tried to remember where Arabia fit into the Middle East. In the playground at school there was a giant map of the world that you could walk on. It was painted on boards, like a dance floor, so you could step from country to country. But because no one bothered to take off their shoes, most of Europe had turned a funny shade of gray. Arabia was yellow, shaped like the body of a bagpipe.

"Go on."

Most Arabs are desert dwellers. The nomads, or Bedouins, live by a strict honor code. As there are many tribes, fighting often breaks out between rival clans. Given the opportunity, they are also notorious raiders.

I wondered if Lawrence ever felt homesick.

"So he joined the Bedouins?"

"I think so. The Arabs needed a leader to unite them, and they chose him. He threw out his English clothes and dressed like one of them. See?" I turned to the first page to show Marlo the black and white photograph of Lawrence in Arabian attire. An ornate dagger gleamed at his waist, the curved handle studded with precious stones. The caption read: *In his silk robes, Lawrence looked like a prophet from a bygone age.* "They even gave him a name: Sidi Laurens." I looked up from the book. "I wish I could do that. Go native and all. And get my very own name. Not just Dom – something foreign sounding!"

"You're silly."

I stifled a yawn. The day was starting to catch up with me, but I was determined to finish another chapter before allowing my eyes to shut.

"What happened next?"

"Lawrence became friends with the son of a powerful Arab prince. His name was Feisal. The two of them planned a defence against the Turks."

"What was it?"

I grinned. "Blowing up the railway, of course! Listen:

'It is claimed that Lawrence destroyed more railway tracks than any other man in the Great War. He even invented a cheeky nickname for placing bombs: he became the world's greatest train wrecker. He even invented a nickname for placing bombs: he called it planting tulips.'"

"Ha, ha. I bet the Turks loved that."

I nodded. "The Arabs loved him.

"'As the column struck out across the desert, young Lawrence, dressed in white robes and mounted on a honey-gold camel, rode in front. Behind him followed a Bedouin poet, who improvised songs about him for the men to sing.'"

"Mmm." Marlo leaned her head on one arm.

"They captured all these Turkish strongholds. Yenbo, then El . . . El Wejh." I shrugged. "Don't know how you say it. Mecca was next. More and more Arab chiefs joined the cause. The English assumed that they were fighting for England, but really they were fighting for a free Arabia."

Marlo's eyes were closed. I pulled the bedspread gently over her shoulders and lay back to finish the chapter.

The Arab army was not like the European armies,
powered by tanks, airplanes, and artillery.
Nevertheless, mounted on racing camels and armed
with scimitars, they fought with a pride and vigor
not witnessed since the days of Mohammed.

It wasn't such a bad book, after all. I might even finish it in the morning.

I fell asleep without remembering to turn off the lamp.

SEVEN

I dreamed that I was on a camel.

The rest of the caravan was trooping across the sand dunes to Aqaba, but I hadn't yet worked out how to make my camel move. She snorted, contemplating the scene with hooded eyes fringed by long, black eyelashes. A robed figure tugged at one of my threadbare reins as he passed, and my mount broke into a trot. Then, a battle cry was raised ahead of us, and I watched in wonder as the pack streamed forth. Faster and faster, the camels galloped, bodies lean, legs stretching farther with each stride, necks straining, heads low, drinking the wind.

I looked down. My camel's large hooves slipped into the loose sand, crumpling it into velvety folds as she shifted her weight from side to side. As her pace lengthened, the rhythm of her gait quickened to a canter. Up and down, so hard that I felt my insides leaping, I bumped heavily against the hard saddle. The more I tried to sit tight, the more roughly her gallop flung me forward and back, forward and back.

A small sandstorm enveloped our party, sending dervish clouds of fine, golden dust swirling above our heads. The pounding of stallion hooves upon the packed earth created a dull roar that cascaded roughly across the plain, rolling and rumbling as if the earth itself was being racked by tremors from deep within.

We edged our way to the front of the pack, hooting and hollering madly, brandishing rifles. The noise was overwhelming.

Shots were fired in the distance, startling the beasts. Snorting and sighing in contempt, my camel stumbled to a halt, tossing me through the air. I tumbled to the ground with a thud, sand filling my mouth and nose. I tried to shout, but the sand made it impossible for any noise to escape.

As I lay there, staring up at the brilliant blue sky, the noises of battle slowly receded. I heard the gentle clatter of my mum washing dishes. A fushia headscarf floated gently across the sky. The sun crept slowly into view, burning out my line of vision with a fierce white glare.

I was staring into the glowing lightbulb when I woke.

"Scared of the dark, are you?" Marlo teased. "You left the lamp on all night."

"What time is it?"

"Don't know. Early. Someone's in the kitchen." She rolled back onto her haunches. "It was really quiet last night."

"I know. Uncle Roo said those Travelers play music, but I didn't hear anything."

"They're too far away."

"I suppose." I chewed my lip. "I wonder what they're like."

Marlo sighed impatiently. "That mask is spooky. I wouldn't want to sleep alone in here if I were you."

"That's because you're a baby. You didn't want to sleep alone in your own room."

Marlo poked her tongue at me. "Did you finish reading that?" She pointed at the green book by my side. It had fallen shut, no marker to indicate how far I'd read.

"Not yet."

My sister paused.

"I miss Mum," she said. "No one came in to wake us up this morning." Marlo had started to play with the tassels on my bedspread. "What do you think she's doing right now?"

"Resting, probably."

She nodded slowly, then sniffed, forcing the tears from dry wells.

"Come on!" I heaved myself out of bed, refusing to give her time to cry.

She looked up at me with wide eyes. "Where are you going?"

"To get some breakfast. Then I'm going to explore outside. Maybe we can go swimming."

She perked up instantly. "I'll get my costume!"

Birdie was cracking eggs into a bowl as we crept into the kitchen. My stomach tensed. I'd been sure it would be Auntie Sylv, organizing a fry-up for us on our first day.

"Good morning," said Marlo shyly, sliding into a chair.

Birdie spun around, and the beads that trimmed her dressing gown jingled merrily. Today she wore a brilliant blue shawl, the same color as Otto's MG. She grinned broadly. "Morning to you, too!" she replied, shuffling over to the stove where butter was melting in a pan. She wore tatty Persian slippers, emerald green with silver sequins. "What will it be, then? Milk? Tea?"

"Tea, please," said Marlo. She glanced at me. "For both of us."

"Coming right up," sang Birdie. "I'm making pancakes."

"Ooh," sighed Marlo.

"Not crepes, sweetie – not what you folks on *this* side of the pond call pancakes. These are Genuine American Griddle Cakes. Fat and fluffy!" She grinned slyly over her shoulder. "Like Otto's books."

"So, Otto writes, and you draw, and the Reverend Cleary makes music?"

"That's the sum of it. None with great success, I might add." She folded a floury mixture in with the

eggs, then began to ladle the batter into the hissing pan.
A sweet buttery smell filled the room. "I've been here
the longest – since Christmas. Cleary arrived early this
year, and Otto came a few weeks later. Time sure flies.
I've not finished half the drawings I'd hoped to."

"Can we see one?"

Birdie paused, considering Marlo with wide eyes.
The gloopy batter began to drip slowly from the ladle.
"Would you like to? They're not really for kids. I'm no
Beatrix Potter, hon."

Marlo shrugged.

"I'll get you one I did in a trance recently," said
Birdie, tapping one finger thoughtfully on the counter-
top. "Dominic – " and she beckoned me over. "Can I
trust you with the pancakes? Just slide a knife under
each one, keep it from burning. I'll be quick as a bunny!"

Aghast, I took the knife from her and peered into
the pan. Three round circles were beginning to bubble
furiously. I poked at one.

Moments later, Birdie reappeared. Under one arm
she carried a long roll of heavy canvas, which she laid
with a thump on the table. I gratefully handed her the
knife, and she nudged me out of the way by the stove.

"I'll take over from here," she said. "You help your
sister unroll that. Careful, mind. Pancakes won't be a
minute!"

Exchanging bemused glances, Marlo and I carefully
unrolled the sheet from one end of the table to the
other. It was about eight feet long, the calico thick and

coarse to touch. The drawings were done in charcoal. That explained her smudged fingers.

I'd never seen anything like it.

Faces. The roll was covered with faces – girls mainly, with delicate features like pixies. Some were smiling, others stared out blankly through huge, dark eyes. The face of one was obscured by a floppy straw hat. There were no empty spaces. Dramatic swirls and flourishes filled the gaps from face to face, like rolling thunder-clouds that carried the figures on the wave of a dream. They were intricate and wild, unnerving – yet I couldn't bring myself to look away.

"Who are they?" whispered Marlo.

"Your guess is as good as mine," laughed Birdie, flopping some pancakes onto a plate. "There," she said with satisfaction, placing them before us. "There's butter and jam, and your uncle's honey, of course – and maple syrup sent over last week from my sister." She busily rolled up the canvas.

"So you just made them up?" persisted Marlo, as I tucked in to my breakfast.

"Certainly not!" Birdie began to serve herself, dousing her pancakes in thick golden syrup. "I saw them all briefly. Took me a few hours to connect with the other side, but they were lively enough when they finally decided to show themselves. One was called Flo. The one in the hat, that is. There were a couple of sisters, Sarah and Lizzie. And an Amelia." She shook her head sadly. "Amelia was very young."

"They weren't Gypsies, were they?" Marlo glanced at me. I could almost hear the skipping rhyme that must have been going through her head:

My mother said
I never should
Play with Gypsies
In the wood
If I did
She would say,
"Naughty little girl to disobey!"

Marlo wasn't much good at skipping, but she sure did love those stupid songs. "My brother wants to meet the people living in the wagons at the bottom of the hill."

"Does he now?" Birdie nodded sagely. "Well, I couldn't tell you about the Romany. They steer clear of me, usually." She chuckled. "No, these girls were as English as crumpets." She chuckled. "Emphasis on *were*."

"Were they all – " Marlo struggled to compose herself, "*dead?*"

"Hogwash and nonsense!"

It was Otto, delivering an uncanny impersonation of the Reverend Cleary. He beamed at our startled expressions.

"Morning, children!"

"Morning, Otto," mumbled Marlo, staring into the pool of syrup that Birdie had poured for her. Talking about dead people had been one thing. Seeing their faces was another. I nudged her nervously with my toe, tried to smile.

"Beautiful day out there," said Otto, pulling up a chair. "It'll be hot as the jungle soon. Reminds me of the Amazon."

"You've been to the Amazon?" asked Marlo.

"Oh, indeed I have," nodded Otto vaguely. "Doing research among the Amahuaca . . . for one of my books."

Birdie sighed loudly.

"I thought it was Mongolia, Otto," she drawled. "Among the Dongxiang."

"That was *later*." He nudged me with his elbow, stacking the remaining pancakes on his plate. "Mongolia was anything but hot!"

Birdie sighed again.

"It changes every time," she muttered. Otto pretended to ignore her.

"When I was your age," he said to Marlo, "I was already cultivating a rather – how shall I put it – a rather *Rubenesque* figure." He patted his belly is if it were a prize pumpkin. "The only thing that kept me from getting pulped by the older lads was my talent for spinning tall tales. I was like whatshisname in *The Arabian Nights* – "

"I think you'll find it was a she," interjected Birdie dryly. "Sheherazade."

"Bless you." Otto grinned smugly. "I'm going to finish my book today," he announced, as Birdie began passing around rashers of bacon. "My best to date."

"What's it about?" asked Marlo.

Otto slurped his coffee loudly and set about tucking into the pancakes. "It's hard to describe," he said at last. "Try to imagine *The Ringer Returns* meets *The Golden Hades* meets *Circumstantial Evidence*." He chewed thoughtfully, working his jaw around a corner of bacon. "It won't surprise you to hear I'm a real Edgar Wallace fan."

"So what happens in it?" Marlo asked.

"It's a kind of spy thriller, action, adventure, whodunit – set in a parallel universe. The main character's a washed-up music hall artist who's being pursed by shape-shifting wolverines."

"Aren't wolverines just a kind of otter?" Birdie smirked. "Maybe you're thinking of wolves, Otto."

"If I was thinking of wolves, I would have said wolves, wouldn't I?"

"You're the boss."

Otto turned back to Marlo.

"The hero's name is Maxx Moriarty. That's Maxx with a double *x*. He's a sort of Robin Hood-Professor Challenger hybrid."

"Is he like Buck Rogers?" Marlo glanced at me. "We listen to Buck Rogers on the wireless all the time at home."

"Like Buck, only better."

The pancakes were like nothing I'd tasted before: almost as good as eating cake for breakfast. For a few minutes, the four of us munched in contented silence.

"You rascals should wander down to the cove," suggested Otto at last.

"On our own?"

Otto shrugged. "Why not? Not much fun with us fogeys tagging along, eh?"

This was something, at least. Marlo looked suspicious.

"I'm not sure Mum would want us going alone," she said, shaking her head. "We might get lost."

I shot her a fierce glare.

"You'll be fine!" Birdie said. "For once, he's said something sensible. Kids should be free. You learn best that way. Just follow the footpath."

I slid from my chair, grabbing Marlo's arm as I passed behind her.

"Ow!" she squealed. "I've not finished!"

"We'll take care of that," laughed Otto, spearing two of Marlo's pancakes with his fork as the door clattered behind us. "I want to hear tales of a ripping adventure tonight!"

EIGHT

"Do you think she *really* sees ghosts?" asked Marlo uneasily, as we clambered down the rocky drive. Blackthorn bushes and tall spires of foxgloves brushed our arms, whispering busily amongst themselves.

"Of course not," I huffed.

"But those drawings – "

"She's just a batty American lady, Marlo. Only a little more batty than the other two."

"I think Otto's funny."

"He's all right." I squinted into the distance. "Look!"

Before us, the green-blue sea stretched to the horizon, soft white waves licking at the thin strip of sandy beach below. A gentle breeze lifted the salty air from the sea to the cliff top, and I inhaled deeply.

"How can we get down there?"

"Follow me."

It took us a while to work our way down the narrow path, out of sight of the house's fat chimney pots and curling gables. Once or twice I stumbled, flailing for slender saplings and protruding bits of bracken to steady myself. I carried the green book in one hand, which made it difficult to balance on the steep descent. Marlo trailed me uncertainly, squealing occasionally as she slipped on loose rocks.

By the time we arrived at the cove, both of us were breathing heavily. The sun had risen in the sky, its dazzling reflection making the waves sparkle as they peaked and dived gently towards us. A seagull drew a wide arc overhead, calling shrilly to his mates.

Marlo gazed wistfully at the horizon. "Ooh. It's lovely."

"Fancy a dip?"

She grinned at me with gleaming eyes. "I'll race you!"

Shoes and socks abandoned, I plunged in headlong. Marlo stumbled to a halt at the water's edge, squealing half with fright and half with giddy joy.

"It's freezing!"

"Don't be a baby!"

"Be *careful,* Dominic."

My sister had never swum properly before in her life, and I'd only been to the coast once, where Dad and I had paddled about for a little while before Dad declared it too cold and forced me out with him. Marlo watched me with a look of elderly concern, fiddling with the strap on her swimming bonnet.

"It's plenty safe, Marlo – just like a bathtub. A big bathtub, that's all!"

Frowning in concentration, Marlo inched in up to her waist.

"Don't go so far!" she pleaded.

"That's it – it's shallow, don't worry."

The smooth stones slid gently beneath our feet, and Marlo yelped with pleasure, eddying with the current. We didn't go in very far, only up to a couple of mossy rocks pointing out of the water about ten yards from land. The cove was protected by a ridge of rocks farther out; beyond them, there was nothing but ocean as far as the eye could see.

We splashed each other until our fingers had turned to raisins, at which point Marlo decided she'd had enough and trudged up to the beach to look for razor shells. I continued scanning the water for signs of life, enjoying the sensation of seaweed gently twirling about my ankles and the smooth, slimy rocks warming my feet. I wondered if I might see the sunfish or turtles Uncle Roo had told me about.

"Dominic!"

I turned to see Marlo's round little figure hunched over something in the sand. She was tracing a pattern with her toe.

"What?"

"Look at this!"

It was a footprint. Or rather, it was a footprint and something else. Not another foot. An indentation.

"It goes up to the cliff," said Marlo.

We followed the trail uncertainly, picking out the footprints with ease – it was a left foot – and always a corresponding groove just a short distance away.

"It ends here," I sighed, staring grimly at the smooth rock face.

"Where'd he go, then?"

"With just one foot, too." I grimaced at her. "Maybe it's a ghost . . ."

"*Don't!*"

I rolled my eyes. "Well, I don't know."

Marlo sternly scanned the beach, hands on hips. "It can't just disappear."

I shrugged, losing interest. "It's probably the Reverend Cleary. He's got a walking stick, remember."

Marlo nodded thoughtfully, unconvinced.

We wandered back.

Home could not have felt farther away. I thought of Lawrence, riding through the desert with his cavalcade of poets and warriors, and I wondered if he ever felt that England had been a dream. That only Arabia was real, because that was where he had come to life.

At the cove, I gathered my towel and draped it over my head. The fluttering white cloth tickled my bare shoulders. Out of the corner of my eye, I caught sight of my shadow – the towel a flowing Bedouin head scarf, brushing the beach's golden slopes. With a smile, I flung myself. to the ground, leaning contentedly against a piece of driftwood and digging my toes into the hot sand. As Marlo busied herself shoveling a hole to China, I flipped through the pages of the green book, trying to find where I'd left off.

> Some of the Arabs were convinced that Lawrence was a prophet, a wise man with magical powers. When a tribe member was thought to have fallen under the evil eye, Lawrence was asked to exorcise the demon. After staring at the man for several minutes, Lawrence declared that the spirit had been driven off. No one questioned him.

I stared at Marlo, imagining myself driving away the evil eye. She must have felt something was up, as she eventually turned around to fix me with a suspicious glare.
"What are you looking at?" she asked.
"Nothing," I replied.
She grunted, unimpressed.

> Once, he disguised himself as an Arab woman to cross into the North Arabian Desert. There, he used his 'tulips' to blow up one of the largest Turkish bridges in Syria, then vanished before he could be spotted.

Vanished. Just like the footprints in the sand.

I gazed out at the sea. *Vanished into the blue.*

"I'm not even close," sighed Marlo. "China's too far away."

We looked at each other, and dissolved into giggles.

There was no reason to suspect that that we were being watched.

NINE

By the end of the first week, I still had not spoken to Birdie, Otto, or the Reverend. They seemed quite happy to gabble away with Marlo at mealtimes, acknowledging my presence, but never forcing me to prove that I was more than a fly on the wall.

It was perfect.

We slowly adjusted to the rhythms of the house, settling in to its rituals and eccentric company. Apart from meals, we were left to ourselves. Uncle Roo was busy converting the old pigeon loft into an artist's studio, and Auntie Sylv spent most of her time visiting wealthy clients who wanted her to paint portraits of their children and pets. The Reverend Cleary was often at church or taking long walks across the moors — sometimes he'd leave early in the morning before anyone else was awake and return as the last dishes were being cleared from supper. Otto and Birdie had colonized the sitting room and the conservatory; they emerged for meals and a few moments of casual banter only when inspiration ran dry.

Marlo and I swam every day. We played hide and seek in the wild, sprawling garden. We bickered. We made up. We spent less time talking about Mum and Dad. One day, Uncle Roo brought us a letter that said the doctors were testing out a new treatment on Mum. It was already working well: she had stopped coughing blood by the end of the second week. If everything went to plan, she'd be on the road to recovery before long. Uncle Roo gave the letter to Marlo, to show to Mum when we returned home. I watched my sister fold it carefully before slipping it between the pages of her cookbook.

I finished reading *Colonel Lawrence and the Revolt in the Desert,* and promptly began to reread it.

"There's plenty more books in the sitting room, you know," Uncle Roo commented one day, adding the final touches to repairs on the wattle fence at the end of the garden. I was perched on his workbench in the shade of an enormous willow tree, lost in the tumult of the Arab Revolt. A couple of my aunt's beloved Silkie hens clucked about our feet, their feather pantaloons ruffled by a gentle breeze.

It was safe to talk; none of the others were around.

"I like this one," I replied at last.

Uncle Roo chuckled. "Just like your sister and that cookbook," he said.

"No it's not," I shot back. "Those are just recipes. This is a real story. Lawrence was a hero – he actually *did* something, Uncle Roo."

Uncle Roo smiled knowingly. I noticed that although his shirt collar and cuffs were badly frayed, they looked somehow right that way. Anywhere else, the tatty edges and threadbare buttonholes would have looked shabby; but out here, on this little patch of moorland overlooking the sea, they seemed somehow . . . well, *earned.*

"I've got to stabilize the wall around the herb garden," he said. "Want to help me find some good stones?"

I leapt to my feet as he began to put away his tools. "Listen!" I insisted. "Listen to this:

'A hundred-mile journey across the Wadi Arabah
leads to the ancient Lost City, impossible to locate
without help from a local guide. The only entrance
is a narrow crevice in the rock face, barely wide
enough for a horse to pass through. Beyond it, the
scene that greets the visitor is one of breathtaking
beauty. Walls carved out of the red-rose mountain
stone are decorated in sumptuous ornaments no less
splendid than the celebrated embellishments of St.
Peter's, Notre Dame or the Taj Mahal. At night, the
pink palace walls seem to glow in the moonlight,
shimmering like silk against a velvet sky.'"

I peered up at him, impatient for a response. Uncle Roo looked slightly taken aback before placing the wooden pegs he was holding on the workbench next to me.

"Petra," he said. "That's Petra you're reading about."

I nodded. "It was the one place in the world that Alexander the Great couldn't conquer, and Lawrence took it in a few days. He held it with the Arabs."

Uncle Roo was watching me very carefully, and I began to feel slightly self-conscious.

"I'd like to go there one day," I mumbled. "It sounds brilliant."

"So it does," replied Uncle Roo. Without another word, he collected the pegs from the workbench and turned away.

It was some kind of magic, that book. It made me feel that anything was possible – that the world was so much bigger than a musty classroom or a damp house in a dirt-poor part of London. I didn't feel trapped inside myself anymore. Behind those green covers, I felt safe.

I still couldn't speak in front of the others. But no one expected me to; I didn't need to.

I just needed my own "Lost City" – and the closest thing to that was the Gypsy camp. Getting there, however, wasn't going to be much easier than journeying all the way to Arabia. When I brought it up with Uncle Roo, he pulled a face and shook his head.

"Your parents wouldn't be too pleased with me if I told them you were fraternizing with Travelers," he'd said. "Don't get me wrong: they're good people. But they're not what you'd expect. They're unpredictable. I don't want you or your sister wandering off near that site – not on your own."

"Will you come with us, then?"

Uncle Roo looked at me almost sadly, as if I was missing the point.

"Not today, Dominic."

I tried asking Auntie Sylv, but she just pursed her lips and looked concerned and told me to ask Uncle Roo.

I would have asked Otto, if I could have spoken to him. He might have driven me down to the campsite in his blue MG. I could have gone and talked to the Romany folk, maybe learned some of their ways like Lawrence did with the Arabs in the desert. There might even be a fellow like Dahoum to teach me their language and help me discover hidden secrets as Lawrence did in Carchemish. Then I'd come back and tell it all to Otto, who would write it down in one of his books. And one day, a boy like me would read that book and think "'Blimey. That Dominic Walker was a brave chap! He must have been real clever to learn them Romany ways and all."

But I still couldn't speak to Otto.

Then I remembered what had happened with Lawrence. The military doctors had tried to stop him signing up for the army – so what did he do? He struck out on his own.

It was that first Sunday morning when I saw my chance. Marlo and I were in the kitchen, setting the table for dinner. We were shaking breadcrumbs from the checkered tablecloth when the Reverend Cleary wandered in.

"Morning, you two," he said, raising one hand in a semi-salute. I no longer panicked when he greeted us; he'd never challenged me to reply.

"Morning, Reverend!" chirped Marlo. "How was church today?"

"Dull as ditchwater," he grumbled, opening the icebox and peering into its sparkling depths. He reached in with one hand and hauled out something in a white cloth. "Something rotten. Stale, stale, stale."

I couldn't tell if he was talking about the sermon or whatever was in the white cloth.

He shuffled over to the table and unwrapped the bundle with painstaking care.

"Do you preach, Reverend?"

The old man shot a curious glance at my sister, bright blue eyes glinting.

"I used to. Not anymore. Ran out of things to say."

"Really, Reverend?" smiled Marlo. She watched him unfold the corners of the white cloth. "What's that?" she asked.

"Pork pie," stated the Reverend. His eyes gleamed. "My wife's finest."

Marlo and I looked at each other.

"You're married, Reverend?" my sister asked.

"Was, my dear. Was. My Annie died almost a year ago."

Marlo had long since abandoned the tablecloth to climb into a chair next to the old gent. So I began folding it myself, glad for something to do.

The Reverend sighed heavily. "But the Good Lord has mercy. By the time she passed away, old Annie had left me nigh fifty pork and apple pies. Bless her."

"*Fifty*, Reverend?" Marlo's eyes widened. He nodded sagely.

"Fifty," he repeated. "I've kept them in the icebox these long months, and have one every Sunday. Down to my last few now. One comes out of the icebox at noon," he glanced at his watch, "and by tea time, it's ready to go into the oven." He unfolded the last section of cloth to reveal a squat, round pastry – slightly gray with frost, crouching expectantly, pasty girth exposed. He placed it gently on a plate.

"There's something rather special about these pies," he said, dreamily. "Rather special."

"Did she make them herself?"

"Of course she did! And not just pork pies, you know." He began to speak quickly, clasping the edge of the table with nervous, bony fingers. "The Westcountry's finest: venison pies, chicken pies, eel pies, steak and kidney pies, leek pies, stargazy pies. Duck pies, too. With glazed orange. Some of them with cranberries. Sausage rolls so flaky you thought you'd gone to heaven."

Marlo nodded eagerly.

"I know the kind you mean," she said, voice hushed. "You know how they get so light and fluffy, don't you?"

"I certainly do *not!*" barked the Reverend. "That's women's secrets." He edged in closer to Marlo, conspiratorial. "But I'd dearly like to know."

Marlo clapped her hands gleefully.

"I'll show you my recipe book!" she said. The kid could hardly contain herself. "You've got to keep the butter cold until the last minute. You can even chill the flour. And you have to mix very, very quickly."

This was it – my chance.

I edged toward the door, waiting for Marlo to swing around and ask where I was going. She didn't. The Reverend was so entranced by her merry babble that he didn't even offer a salute. In an instant, I'd escaped.

It didn't take long to get down to a plateau on the hill, where the bend in the road offered a sheltered view of the valley below. I'd never ventured so far from the house, which was a world unto itself, high up on the cliff with its garden and its long, winding drive and the secret cove at the bottom of the footpath.

The painted wagons were still there. Thin wisps of smoke coiled from the chimney of one of the larger wagons. A man was sitting on its front step, raising a pipe to his mouth and then tipping it at the ground in a slow, practiced way.

I decided to get a little closer. Halfway between myself and the wagons, on the incline, was a copse of trees – elm and sycamore. I knew their names because

Uncle Roo used Cornish elm to build chairs for the garden, and the pale floorboards in the sitting room were made from sycamore. He and Auntie Sylv had hewn the wood from this very glen. That made it almost as good as ours. I scuttled forward.

From the wood, it was possible to see more of the camp itself. A couple of horses grazed lazily in a makeshift enclosure. A dog ambled past them, long pink tongue lolling out of the side of its mouth. Beyond, three women were lining up barrels for washing – plates were going into one, women's dresses into another, and men's shirts and breeches into a third. They used a bowl to rinse their hands and splash their faces as the heat of the sun grew stronger and beat down upon the clean clothing that had already been draped over some lavender bushes to dry. Scrap metal was scattered in piles next to some of the caravans, waiting to be sorted. The man gazed into the distance, tapping his pipe occasionally against his boot before placing it back between his teeth.

Shrill cries drew my attention to a clearing at the edge of the wood where a group of very young children were playing on a blanket of bluebells. The littlest ones wore no clothing. A tall girl with serious eyes carried a baby whose face was as broad and brown as a coffee bean. The girl slung the baby casually on one hip, like a bundle of groceries. A couple of little boys chased each other giddily around her, while she remained as motionless as a maypole, ignoring the infant's grizzling.

I didn't know what to do next, how to involve myself in their activity. Part of me wanted them to spot me, so that I might be invited to join in the game. Part of me wanted to run.

I didn't get a chance to do either.

The last sound I heard before hitting the ground was a fierce *crack*. An instant later, I realized that something had struck the back of my legs, making them buckle beneath me. That was the last thing I remember. The pain came later.

TEN

The cries of children at play had been replaced by the eerie wail of a lone seagull. Perhaps it had strayed too far inland and was thirsty for the salty spray of the cliffs. After a while, it ceased – and then there was nothing but a gentle breeze ruffling the treetops and the distant churning of the sea.

Snapdragons nodded among the bluebells as I rolled onto my side, slowly lifting my head from the sweet smelling earth. Bits of dirt stuck to my face, and I spat out fragments of crushed leaf that had found their way into my mouth.

As I bent my knees to sit up, a sharp pain shot up the backs of my legs, making me cry out. That was when I remembered: someone else was there. I glanced from left to right, scanning the forest for a face.

"What are you looking for, *gadjo?*"

I spun around, flipping myself onto my stomach like a seal.

She stood behind me, hands on hips, head cocked to one side. Her square, boyish face was framed by raggedly cropped brown hair. Her wide mouth was pulled into a smirk; her black gaze piercing. She wore a tattered smock shirt and long blue shorts that brushed the tops of mud-caked Wellington boots.

I felt myself go red, and tried to breathe deeply.

"I'm talking to you, gadjo!" she barked. She was no older than I, but she spoke with the brusque authority of a young man. In fact, she could have made a strikingly handsome boy, with that stubborn chin and square teeth, and a nose that was turned up at the end.

I opened my mouth and felt my tongue catch at the back of my throat.

What's a gadjo? I wanted to say. *I'm just me. Dominic. My Uncle Roo and Auntie Sylv live in the house on the hill.* I realized just how pathetic that would have sounded and clamped my mouth shut.

"You were spying on my sister," she continued. "I saw you."

I shook my head.

"Don't lie, boy. You look at her again, and I'll cut your eyes out, see?"

I nodded vigorously.

The girl began to wander around me. I noticed that one of her legs didn't bend the way the other did. She must have sensed me staring.

"You looking at this now, eh?" and she rolled up one of her shorts. Her leg was brown and covered in scratches. It was surprisingly muscular. Girls aren't supposed to have muscles like that. She laughed at my shocked expression. "Or this one?"

She thrust the other foot in my face, holding the filthy boot just inches from my nose.

It was made of wood.

The lower half of her right leg was – well, it wasn't there. Instead, a smooth wooden rod had been bound with cloth strips just above the kneecap, disappearing into the boot like a shrunken tree poking from an empty pot.

She lowered herself and squatted next to me, hands folded casually over her knees.

"What's your name?" she said, quietly this time. She frowned at my silence, shrugged, then reached out to touch my hair. I flinched, tensing.

"Your hair is like sand," she stated.

She was toying with me, the same way the bullies did back home. Ever since coming to Cornwall, I'd almost forgotten what it felt like – but now the panic came flooding back, pulsing at my temples and my chest and my stomach, just like it used to.

I gulped, trying to look fierce, but secretly terrified that she'd lash out. It was obvious that this girl could make mincemeat of me. I waited.

"How old are you?"

I tried to imagine how I must look through her eyes:

pale and crumpled, gray socks curled about my skinny ankles.

"I thought you might be a poacher, but you're just a boy," she continued, when it was clear I wasn't going to answer. "It's a good thing, too, or else I'd have taken a proper kick at you."

I'm not just a boy. I'm a Bedouin spy. I was planting tulips—

I wanted to tell her that I was here on Colonel Lawrence's orders. That he'd asked me to befriend the people in the wagons; that it was a mission of state importance. *I'm a freedom fighter.*

The girl scowled. "Who was with you on the beach?" she asked. "Was it your sister? Do you have a sister?"

I nodded, slowly.

"I know what you're thinking. You're thinking *So that explains the footprints in the sand.* You're clever, gadjo." She was smiling. Not sneering, just smiling. "I wasn't wearing boots then. I like walking on the beach. Alone. Away from all of them." She sighed softly. "I didn't know you were coming – I climbed a tree. You know the big one, hanging out of the cliff?"

I nodded. How had we missed her?

"I watched you for a long time. Your sister looks like Shirley Temple."

This was becoming more unreal by the minute.

She laughed. "I bet you're thinking *What does a dirty Gypsy know about the cinema?* Aren't you, gadjo?" She shrugged. "I've never been to the cinema. But I've seen posters, in the towns. *Bright Eyes*, right?"

I nodded again. Despite myself, I was still staring at her leg.

"My father trades horses," she said hurriedly. "If I'd been a boy, I would be working with him by now." She pointed to her boot. "When I was three, one of his mares trampled me. I almost died."

I wondered if her father was the man with the pipe.

"I can't ride. The horses are so strong, very fast – you should see them gallop. . . ." Her voice grew wistful as she gazed out to the meadows. Then she looked back at me, grinning defiantly. "But I can do lots of other things." She heaved herself to her feet. "Can you do this?" And she flipped herself onto her hands, feet sticking straight up in the air. She turned a circle and kept her balance for several seconds before bending her legs and standing up.

I shook my head.

"Can you do this?" And she leapt up, grabbing hold of a branch with both hands, swinging herself two or three times before locking her good leg over the branch and heaving herself up to the next one. In a matter of seconds, she was at the top of the tree. I stared in awe. Tree climbing was not something we learned to do in the city.

The girl clambered down, landing with a bump on the ground next to me.

"Why don't you say anything?" she demanded. "Are you stupid? Did they show you a mirror when you were a baby? *Hai shala* – don't you understand?"

I nodded.

"Speak!" she said, beginning to lose patience. "Say something, then!"

Enough. I heaved myself to my feet, wincing as a hot flash of pain seared my legs. I could still walk, just.

"Where are you going, gadjo?"

Home. I'm going home.

The girl was starting to look sheepish. "I didn't mean to hurt you so bad," she said softly. "It's just – my sister." She shrugged. "You were spying on us."

She held my gaze for a moment before sticking out one hand. "My name's Sancha," she said.

Even without gold coins woven through her hair, there was a wildness to Sancha that satisfied me: she was a real Gypsy.

"We're Roma," she explained. "The gadje call us Gypsies."

My blank expression must have made her realize that I hadn't the faintest idea what she meant.

"*Gadje* means 'white people.' Strangers. Outsiders. See?"

I nodded. Sancha had steadied me as I walked, talking all the way until we arrived at the cove. Now, we perched side by side on the bit of driftwood on the beach.

"The gadje are *moxado* – unclean," she explained, matter-of-factly. "You have toilets inside your houses, where you cook food. It's filthy."

I frowned. The only person to tell me I was filthy was Mum, after we'd been playing in the mud slides, or at football in the street.

"Yes, it is," continued Sancha. "Your women give birth in big hospitals, and immediately everyone crowds around to see the baby. Don't you know that's unclean?"

I shrugged. Suddenly, I recalled something written about Lawrence – the desert was clean, he said. He liked it because it felt clean.

"What does your father do?" demanded Sancha.

I looked down and shrugged again.

"Doesn't he do anything?" she persisted. I shook my head. Slowly, I traced a picture in the sand. A rifle.

"A gun? He's a soldier?"

I nodded halfheartedly.

"Is he dead?"

I shook my head slowly.

"A lot of Rom were used in the white war," Sancha reflected. "A lot of them died. Our family in Europe – a lot of them. So stupid! The whites fighting between themselves, thinking they're all so different, good against bad. Huh!" She smiled bitterly. "You know, to us, you're all the same."

We sat in silence for what seemed an age. Finally, Sancha stood up.

"I should go back," she said. "I'll help you to the road."

As we emerged from the footpath, the sound of someone approaching made Sancha stand erect, tense. There wasn't time to run.

It was Marlo.

"Dominic!" she exclaimed. She looked at Sancha, mouth agape. "Who's that?"

Sancha smiled at me.

"Dominic?" she said, thoughtfully, lingering over each syllable. "Dominic." She slapped me on the shoulder, comradely. "*Kushti ratti*, Dominic."

And before Marlo could object, she was gone – black boots scuffing at the dry earth until all trace of her had faded.

ELEVEN

I told Marlo everything – it would have been impossible not to. Then I made her promise not to utter a word about Sancha to the grown-ups.

"But do you think she'll come back?" she asked.

"No – not here. She thinks we're dirty," I replied.

Marlo wrinkled her nose. "*We're* dirty! Did you see her hair?"

As the house gathered for supper that evening, I felt certain that Uncle Roo would know just by looking at me that I'd disobeyed him. Squeezed between my sister and Auntie Sylv at the table, I tried to be even more invisible than usual.

"Where's the Reverend?" asked Marlo, as Birdie nudged slices of corned beef onto her plate.

"He's not feeling very well," sighed Auntie Sylv. "Came home early from Evensong, the poor man. It's the first time he hasn't had the energy to go stomping about the moors after the service."

"He's been losing steam these past few weeks," observed Birdie.

My uncle nodded gravely, stroking his thin silver mustache. "Sounds as if he missed quite the skirmish outside the church tonight," he said.

"What's that, then?" asked Otto, smothering the baked potato before him with lashings of thick, yellow butter. "Nothing to do with his latest musical master-piece, was it?"

Uncle Roo shook his head. "Some of the people in the village are making noises about the Gypsy camp," he said.

Marlo cut me a pointed look, which I tried to ignore. I reached for the bread, taking care to tear it between the fingers of my right hand. Earlier that day, I'd read that eating with the left hand was frowned upon in Arab countries.

"Noises?" asked Birdie. "What kind of noises?"

"Bad ones," said Uncle Roo. "There have been one or two burglaries lately. Some of the women have been into the town with their children, begging. The rumor mill is in full swing, I'm afraid. Some of the ladies in the choir are planning a petition for eviction."

"What's that?" asked Marlo, in a whisper. I wished that she wouldn't look so concerned.

"It means that they want to force them to leave. For good," explained Otto, with a grunt. "Miserable old busybodies."

Uncle Roo shook his head. "These are hard times," he said, more to himself than anyone else. "First, that character Mosley with his blackshirt thugs, trying to turn London upside down with fascist talk. Just like that wretched little German . . . what's his name? Hitler." He poked a well in his creamed spinach, letting the thin green juices drain into the center. "We think we're so lucky here, living beyond all of that. But it's arrived on our doorstep."

"What has, Uncle Roo?" interrupted Marlo, confused.

"He means *prejudice,* sugarpie," explained Birdie. "Fearful folks, lashing out at an easy target." She adjusted her scarf irritably. "Those poor people have been coming here for hundreds of years. And they can't defend themselves. Makes you ashamed."

"Well, they don't make it easy for themselves," Otto said. "They do choose to live outside normal society – "

"No more than we do!" exclaimed Birdie. "We, more than anyone else, should know what it's like to be outsiders. We're *all* outsiders." She jerked her chin at me. "Even these two kids." She heaped more baked beans onto her plate, the steaming red-brown pile sludging its way in all directions. "If you ask me, those people have got something right, at least. They don't settle for 'normal.' They're free."

"Not for long, it seems," sighed Uncle Roo. "It looks as if they're going to be moved off that land sooner rather than later."

We ate in silence for several minutes before Marlo piped up again. I wanted to kick her, honestly I did.

"What if we could help them?" she asked.

Auntie Sylv smiled indulgently.

"That's a lovely idea, Marlo," she said. "But this isn't the kind of thing children ought to get involved in. It's complicated."

I groaned inwardly. Typical grown-up talk.

Sitting on the porch later that evening with a plate of macaroons between us, watching the sun sink into the sea, I remembered what Lawrence had said when someone asked him why he'd joined the Arab Revolt.

"*I liked a particular Arab,*" he'd replied, "*and thought that freedom for the race would be an acceptable present.*"

He was talking about Dahoum. When Lawrence left the archaeological dig at Carchemish, he placed his friend in charge and vowed that he would win the war for him. He wrote to Dahoum, *I drew these tides of men into my hands and wrote my will across the sky in stars to earn you Freedom, that seven-pillared worthy house . . .*

But when the war ended, Lawrence found out that Dahoum had died in 1916 – too early to see the Arab lands liberated. Lawrence was devastated.

I tried to picture Sancha: her tanned, square face and blazing eyes, those muddy black Wellingtons, that wooden, lifeless leg she'd used to swing herself into the treetops. What was she doing right now, as I watched the fireflies darting busily about the garden?

She'd called me gadjo. Outsider.

In my dream, sand was everywhere, indistinguishable from the ground or the sky, lashing my skin with spiteful venom. Over the human commotion, the animals brayed in fear. Slowly, very slowly, my camel and I followed the wind, heads lowered, staggering beneath the gusting pressure from behind. Deafened by the shrieking gale and blasting sands, we stumbled upon soft dunes that swallowed us up to our waists and across the hard slate plateau that burned under the midday sun.

By the time the storm finally ceased, blasted stumps of desert shrubs struggled to emerge from beneath a heavy blanket of sand, pointing the route forward in a hundred different directions. My mouth was so dry that it felt as if my tongue had turned to stone; my clothes crackled as I moved.

Someone was approaching us – a tiny desert specter. A fine coat of golden dust covered her from head to toe. She seemed to be carried aloft by the shimmering heat, and only when she stood above me, was I certain that she was not a ghost.

At first she seemed happy to see me, and I was filled with relief. But then her expression darkened.

"Why don't you say anything?" she challenged.

What do you want me to say? screamed the voice in my head.

"Anything!" she shouted. "Say anything!"

And then she vanished, and I was alone once more.

TWELVE

I t was several days before I saw her again.

We had just returned from a shopping excursion in St. Ives and had stopped in Zennor so that Auntie Sylv could pay Uncle Roo's tab at the pub. There wasn't a crowd outside the church anymore, but I did notice a bit of paper fluttering on the parish notice board. PROTECT YOUR COMMUNITY AGAINST THE VAGRANT THREAT it blared, but Auntie Sylv had hurried us on so quickly that I couldn't read what else was written below.

She'd bought me a pair of canvas plimsolls, much lighter than the battered leather shoes I wore year-round at home. Marlo got a new sundress that was yellow with pink flowers and just short enough that it pouffed when she did a twirl. Right now, she was rushing home with Auntie Sylv to show it to the Reverend. They were going to bake a rhubarb pie together that afternoon.

It was good to walk alone for a bit, testing out my new shoes. I clenched my toes, gripping the rough ground through the thin rubber soles. I could be a tennis player in those plimsolls – or even better, an Olympic sprinter! Mum and Dad would say Auntie Sylv shouldn't have; they'd cost too much. But by then it would be too late to do anything about it.

Sancha was alone, leaning against a mossy boulder in a field on the other side of the camp. A tiny white creature was in her lap, bony legs splayed awkwardly in four different directions, bleating and struggling as the girl tried to guide a bottle to its mouth.

My first instinct when I saw her was to call out. As usual, I faltered; it might attract attention. Even up in the house, people might hear me – then they'd come running, and fuss and chatter, and make a big show over what an achievement it was. Or worse, someone else might hear – one of the villagers out for a stroll, or even a Gypsy driving a mule and wagon down the dusty road. And then they'd look at me, and I'd have to acknowledge them, or maybe even introduce myself.

And by that time, she might be gone.

I tiptoed lightly across the grass, concentrating on the sheep droppings scattered about the field like so many tiny nuggets of coal. Enjoying the soft squelch of my new shoes, I skirted two cow pats and a ditch before reaching a crest of the hill.

The lamb must have sensed my presence before she did because it stopped struggling just long enough to stare up at me with wide, apprehensive eyes. Then it squealed again, and kicked furiously.

Sancha turned quickly. When she saw that it was only me, she allowed herself a slightly embarrassed smile. As she rose, I noticed that she clutched a long line of string tied in a collar around the lamb's neck.

"Dominic," she said, grinning lazily. "Where'd you come from?"

I pointed to the road.

"From town?" she asked, the shadow of a scowl passing over her face. "What are the gadje planning? The *Rom Baro* told us there was a scene at the church the other night. You know about that?"

I shook my head again, hoping to reassure her.

She grunted.

"Every few years, this happens," she said. "They never do anything."

There's a petition, I wanted to say. *It's not just rumors this time. The whole town is uniting against you. They're trying to do something.*

"And every year, my father says this will be the last time. We won't come back." Sancha shook her head with a knowing smile. "But we always do."

She pointed to the lamb.

"See what I found?" she said. "Stuck in the stream on the other side of the forest, making such a racket. The farmer there accused my father of poaching, once — but he can't even look after his own animals, so what good is that, huh?" She shook the bottle at me. "I was trying to feed her. But she's so stupid. Doesn't know I'm only trying to help."

I knelt on the ground and stretched out one hand. Curious, the tiny creature stumbled toward me, sniffed my fingers, and then gently poked at them with its rough, pink tongue. Its eyes were like pearl buttons, the pupils obscured by milky swirls that made me wonder if it could see properly.

"See, she *is* hungry!" exclaimed Sancha. "What's wrong with milk, you silly thing? You'd rather eat *him?*"

She grinned at me, and I smiled back.

"Come on," said Sancha. She tugged at the lamb's lead, making off down the hill once more. After a moment, she turned around.

"Want to see my fort?" she asked. It sounded like a challenge, but I was getting used to her abruptness. I promptly slid after her, forgetting all about my new plimsolls.

Sancha whistled loudly as she led us over the moor, jerking the lamb to heel whenever it threatened to wander off in the wrong direction. Tripping knock-kneed after her, it bleated plaintively.

"If you get lost around here, we'll never see you again, you dumb animal!" she said hotly. "There's no way someone as thick as you could get home all on your own."

The land was now as flat as a desert steppe – rugged and barren and eerily quiet. Overhead, bruised clouds hung heavy in the sky. It was no longer possible to hear the comforting rumble of the sea. I glanced around, trying to judge the distance we had traveled.

"Don't worry," said Sancha. "It's not far now. I know my way."

On first appearance, her "fort" looked to be nothing more than a pile of rocks dropped at random in the most lonely, desolate spot you could imagine. In reality, it turned out to consist of three enormous boulders – easily ten feet high – pinned against each other to make a sort of pyramid. They formed a tented frame on which one large slab had been laid to complete the roof. Bits of gorse had been crammed in to fill the spaces beneath the capstone, squeezing out any light that chanced to filter through.

"It's not really mine," explained Sancha. "It's been here forever. I just stuck in the grass to keep it from leaking when it rains, see?"

I nodded enthusiastically.

"You can go inside, if you like," she said.

There wasn't much room – just enough for the two of us, and the lamb. The damp ground had been dug out to make a hollow toward the back.

"I think it used to be some sort of burial ground," said Sancha, indicating the rich, black earth piled up at the back of the cave. "My father says that once upon a time, there were many of these all over the country. They were used for ancient rituals."

She sat down, hauling the reluctant lamb into her lap once more.

"When I was little, I spent a whole night out here with my sister. We'd run away – you know, like everybody does." I nodded, even though I'd never run away before. "When our father found us, he gave us such a beating!" She laughed. "I couldn't sit down for days."

I tried to picture my own father, frowning over the papers back home. Whenever my friends and I had been up to no good – nicking sweets from the local shop, say – we'd have to keep an eye out for the dads returning from work on the docks. Some of those dads were right fearsome creatures. Not ours, though. I don't think he'd have known what to do if he'd caught me stealing. He'd probably just look sad and shake his head – which is almost worse than getting a thrashing, now that I think about it.

Sancha was pointing the milk bottle at the lamb once more, to no avail.

"My sister doesn't come out with me much anymore," she said, quietly. "Not since she turned fourteen. She thinks that because she's getting married this year, she's suddenly all grown up." She stroked the lamb gently as it nuzzled her elbow. "It's all right, I suppose. She used to try and protect me from the others, when they made fun of my leg. Now I can look after myself." And she knocked firmly on her boot, as if to prove its resilience.

The lamb had finally taken the bottle in its mouth, and it drank hungrily. Sancha smiled in satisfaction.

"You know, we're not so different, gadjo," she reflected, after a pause. "I lost my leg; you've lost your voice. But I can sure use this old stump when I need to, eh?" She grinned wickedly. "*Ov yilo isi?* Does your knee still hurt?"

I shook my head. The black-blue bruise had turned yellow in the last few days; the pain had long since disappeared.

"Tha's good," she whispered, more to the tiny creature in her lap than to me.

I wished that I could have said something – I would have asked her a question, because girls like to be asked about themselves – but the more I wanted to, the harder it became. In the end, we just sat there.

By the time we finally emerged, the shape of the land had turned black against a steel sky. Trudging across the moor, Sancha cradled the lamb in her arms while I stumbled a few paces behind, far less certain of the darkness passing silently beneath my feet. At last we reached the road that would take us our separate ways.

"They wouldn't be pleased if they found out I spent time with you," said Sancha. "The *kumpania*. They don't know any better. Especially now, with all the anger – the adults spend a lot of time talking about it. . . ." Her voice trailed off.

I nodded, staring at the ground.

"Sounds like you do, too. Eh?" She stared up at the hill, and I wondered what she must have made of the sprawling sandstone house. For a moment, I was tempted to invite her back to meet the others. They would be enchanted by her strangeness, and she by our modern, cluttered lives. When Lawrence brought his Arab friend, Dahoum, on a visit to England in 1913, the boy had been amazed by running water and the Underground trains. In turn, he had amazed locals by riding a bicycle through Oxford in his flowing robes.

But Sancha beat me to it. "You'd better get home quick."

I might just have managed it, then, as she began to saunter off. I might just have shouted something. Like *"Thanks."* Or *"Maybe I could help you fix up the fort tomorrow."*

Or even *"I'm sorry I can't do something. Lawrence would have. But blowing up the railways isn't going to help much, all the way out here."* I didn't get a chance to. She was gone before I could decide what it was I might say.

Moments later, my attention was distracted by a little figure hurtling down the hill from the house, tumbling through the semi-darkness in a flurry of sobs.

"Dominic!" cried Marlo, crumpling into my arms. "Come quickly. It's the Reverend!"

THIRTEEN

He had collapsed in the kitchen.

My sister shouted for the others, and Uncle Roo and Otto had managed to get the old man upstairs and into bed. A doctor was with him now.

The six of us waited gloomily in the sitting room – silent, but for Marlo, who had broken into hiccups from the shock of it. Auntie Sylv hadn't even noticed that my brand-new plimsolls were smudged with grass stains.

"I'm sure he'll be fine," she said, her voice pitched too high.

"The old codger's seen worse than this," said Uncle Roo.

No one replied. Birdie coughed quietly into her shawl, eyes lowered.

"Isn't it time the children were in bed?" muttered Otto.

"It's too early!" protested Marlo. Her little face was pale and strained; almost unrecognizable. She looked up to me, searchingly, and I squeezed her clammy hand. Who knew what she was feeling just then? He had been her first real friend – different from me, from the grown-ups who fussed over her back home.

Every second that passed, punctuated by the steady *tick-tick-tick* of the grandfather clock, felt like a minute. One. Two. Three.

Four.

Five.

At last, the doctor's brisk steps brought us all to our feet. "It's his heart."

The doctor was a shrunken man, with a head too large for the rest of his body, a small, pointed beard and the thinnest of mustaches, which parted like a broken twig over his upper lip. His shirt collar was crumpled and he fiddled with his trouser pockets. He peered evenly at Uncle Roo through tiny wire spectacles.

"What about it?" asked Uncle Roo.

"It's very weak," sighed the doctor. "Barely audible."

Auntie Sylv tried to herd me and my sister toward the door.

"Otto's right," she whispered. "Time for bed, you two."

"But I want to see the Reverend!" pleaded Marlo. "Please, Auntie Sylv – "

The doctor pursed his lips, the coarse hairs on his chin shifting almost imperceptibly. He knew something we didn't; I could tell just by looking at him. Sometimes, you don't need to speak to make your thoughts clear.

"It might be just as well," he said, glancing from Auntie Sylv to Uncle Roo. "Just a quick visit. He's awake."

That was enough for Marlo. She shot ahead of us, out of that room and up the stairs like a bolt.

At first we thought he was asleep – or worse. He lay very still, eyes closed, arms folded serenely on his chest. The kerosene lamp was turned down low, and shadows nestled against the curtains and around the bed. It was a simple, snug room: not bright and airy like ours, filled with curiosities and fresh flowers; or like Birdie's, which smelled of perfume and powder; or like Otto's, which was scattered with glossy magazines and unsheathed records. This room was dark and plain, with just a wooden crucifix on one wall next to the washstand. On the desk lay an open notebook, and through the dim light I could see that the pages were covered in a spidery scrawl.

Marlo pressed up against the bed, stretching on tiptoe to speak into his ear.

"Reverend Cleary? Are you awake?" she whispered.

His eyelids fluttered open.

"What's that, my dear?" he said, hoarsely. "What are you doing up here? You should be watching the oven."

Marlo shook her head.

"I didn't finish the pie, Reverend," she said. "The rhubarb's done stewing, though. It's all ready for you when you feel better."

A faint smile brought the slightest flush of color to his cheeks. Then again, it might just have been the shadows playing games.

"I'd like you to do something for me," he said.

"Anything, Reverend!"

He spoke so softly it was a wonder she could hear a word of it.

"The Larkspur Festival is in two weeks' time," he said. "Annie never missed a Fair, all the years we were married. And as far back as I can remember, she won the top prize at the baking stall. Always."

"I'm listening, Reverend."

He coughed fitfully, and was silent for several moments – worn out, I suppose.

"That prize should be yours this year. You'll do that for me? And for Annie?"

Marlo's whole body tightened with apprehension.

"I can't promise that, Reverend – I've never baked anything on my own. . . ."

"You'll do that for me, won't you? Promise me."

Marlo looked at him in amazed silence. Then, not sounding at all like her usual self, she murmured, "Yes, Reverend. I promise."

I wasn't expecting what came next.

"Dominic – is your brother there?"

Me?

I shuffled forward.

"Is that you, Dominic Walker?"

I nodded.

"He's here, Reverend," squeaked Marlo.

The Reverend sighed.

"I want to tell you something, Dominic," he said. "About that book you're always hiding behind."

I glanced down at Marlo, who was too busy sniffling into the bedsheets to pay attention.

"We all need our heroes, Dominic," continued the Reverend. "When we're old, and we realize the time that's been wasted. . . ." he coughed feebly. "When I was your age, I dreamed of traveling to the Congo and converting the natives. My plan was to collect butterflies in between baptisms – " Another cough. "Would that my youthful zeal had endured!"

Marlo hiccupped loudly, and the old man steadied her with a gentle hand.

"I took my God for granted," he continued. "Then He left me high and dry: a lonely country pastor who writes awful music for old ladies to massacre. With nothing but fifty pies to show for my life."

"No, Reverend–" begged Marlo, clasping his hand tightly.

"I knew the man you've been reading about – " and the Reverend turned to fix me with a clear, blue stare. "Ned Lawrence. He hated the books that were written about him. Every one of them. Thought them vulgar!"

I felt my stomach turn.

"'To have news value is to have a tin can tied to one's tail,' he said. They stalked him like a prize boar when he came back from India." The Reverend's breathing grew

shallow, and for a moment I thought that he was asleep –
but no. "Lawrence was a complex man," he sighed. "A
wise man. He knew his place in that war: he knew the
difference between helping the Arabs and trying to fight
their battles for them. He knew that the seeds of future
wars would be sown in Arabia."

The Reverend began to press himself forward on his
elbows in an effort to sit up.

"No, Reverend," whispered Marlo. "You have to rest."

The old man acquiesced with a small grunt of irritation. "He was always fascinated by the Crusades. . . .
You'll know that, of course," he said at last, still looking
at me. "Lawrence was enamored of chivalry, heroism –
all the old ideals – and yet he hated killing. His favorite weapon was the Colt Peacemaker revolver. The
Peacemaker! I held it with my own two hands."

I stiffened. Could it possibly be true?

"It was years ago, now. Lawrence was visiting friends
in Cornwall, just after the war ended. It wasn't the first
time he'd been here, mind." The shadow of a smile
momentarily brightened his creased features, which
had turned as gray as a stone. "When he was a lad, he'd
run away from home and tried to join the Royal
Garrison at St Mawes. . . ."

We waited for him to continue.

"But the second time was after the war. Lawrence had
an infected wound which began to haemmorage, and I
was called in to perform the last rites. . . ." The Reverend
closed his eyes, frowning in concentration. "He believed

in God, you know. Didn't think much of the church – his parents were evangelists, you see. I suppose that put him off – but he had his own faith. The hemorrhage turned out not to be fatal, but he wasn't to know at the time. He poured his heart out to me."

Marlo glanced from the Reverend to me.

"What did he say?" she asked.

"He was angry . . . let down. He lost someone in that war, he felt he'd betrayed him. He said that he'd buried it. A gift of some sort. He wanted to forget."

Marlo looked up at me blankly, cheeks glistening with sticky tears.

"After he left, I started to look for it. I think it was something to do with the Arabs, with Feisal and that lot. They were let down after the war – all the things he'd promised them, taken away." The old man's body rocked with a cold shudder. "I wasted my life giving dull sermons on Leviticus," he whispered. "I thought I might learn to believe – that's why I searched for it. And now, I think I know . . . the gravesite . . ."

My mind raced. Was he delirious?

"Take it," gasped the Reverend, whose voice had grown thin. "It mustn't just lie there, waiting to be dug up by accident if that land sells. It should go to someone who needs it. We all need hope, Dominic. Don't settle to dream by night. The dreamers of the day are dangerous men . . ."

I don't remember what happened next. Vague words; a soft, tired wheezing sound.

"Children?" Auntie Sylv had appeared at the door, silhouetted against the soft light flooding in from the hallway. "Rupert . . ."

The rest of that night is a blur. The clanging of an ambulance; the mournful expression of the doctor; Uncle Roo's haggard face; Birdie's drawn with tears. Otto wandered out alone into the balmy dusk, forgetting to shut the door behind him.

And all the while, Marlo clung to me – fierce with sorrowful rage, tiny fingers digging into my arms like daggers.

FOURTEEN

The funeral was pretty simple; just our eccentric little crew and a smattering of townspeople. I don't suppose we were more than twenty in all.

It was just as well, really. The church – which seemed enormous from the outside, all gray and square and medieval looking, and starting to slump in the middle like a cake that hadn't risen properly – was actually very small. The carved wooden pews creaked with the slightest movement, so I ended up sitting ramrod straight through most of the service.

The ladies' choir sang an introduction that sounded something like a convoy of trains screeching to an emergency stop. With the exception of one or two hymns, all of the music in the order of service was by the Reverend. It was difficult to say whether or not it was any good, through the earnest shrilling of all those

elderly voices rising over the tinny clatter of the organ.
I tried to believe that they were doing him proud.

"Peregrine Albert Cleary, although he lived in
Cornwall all his life, was a man of global vision," boomed
the vicar, leaning rather too heavily against the sighing
lectern. "Those who knew him well were limited to a
select and treasured few. But they will all attest to his clear
insight, and deep understanding of the Good Book."

Birdie laid a gentle hand on my sister's knee. The
poor kid hadn't spoken all morning.

The vicar smacked his lips and shifted his weight.
"For Peregrine, born and raised near Mousehole, and a
member of this parish for most of his life, Palestine was
no farther away than the nearest village. The Sea of
Galilee was always within easy reach, as close to hand
as Zennor Cove."

Otto coughed loudly.

"In the final months of his life, living with friends
on nearby Medina Hill, we might imagine him casting
his eyes across these green cliffs, and feeling what Moses
felt on sighting the Promised Land . . ."

I turned my attention to the wooden Jesus above the
altar. He was nailed to a cross that had been suspended
at an angle from the ceiling, so it looked a bit as if he
was flying over the congregation. Just two weeks ago,
Marlo had told the Reverend that I'd called her a baby
for being too afraid to dunk her head when we'd gone
swimming. I'd half expected the Reverend to tell me off,

but instead, he simply smiled. "Someone once told me that we should nail all our fears to the cross," he told her. In retrospect, it seemed like strange advice to give, seeing as Jesus seemed to be struggling enough as it was.

I allowed my gaze to wander the streaked, ancient walls dotted with memorial plaques. No fewer than five had been polished to a high sheen, and it didn't take me long to realize that they were all dedicated to local men who had died in the war.

My thoughts began to retrace the Reverend's strange last words. What had he been searching for all these months, this "gift" that Lawrence said he'd buried? I caught myself and marveled at my predicament: opportunities such as this simply didn't come to boys like me. A month ago, I would never have believed that I'd be crossing paths with a true hero. Perhaps history didn't work in a straight line, after all; perhaps it weaved through itself, plaiting together lives even after they had ended. Perhaps I was standing at a knot in history, a knot that only I could untangle. If that was the case, a great responsibility had landed on my shoulders.

Whatever the treasure was, it must have been important to have meant so much to the Reverend. Could it be valuable? A key to the Lost City, perhaps? Or perhaps it was something dangerous. He had mentioned the Peacemaker revolver. Was it a weapon? An amulet to ward off the evil eye? I pressed my thumbnail into the soft, woody flesh of the pew, itching to know the answer.

At last, here was my chance to share in Lawrence's mystery, to become a part of his legend: all I had to do was reach out and grab it.

During the final hymn, I felt Marlo begin to rock gently at my side. As the coffin was carried down the aisle, Auntie Sylv sniffed loudly, her face pinched and tired. Otto grimly passed her his handkerchief.

I will not cease from mental flight,
nor shall my sword sleep in my hand,
Till we have built Jerusalem
in England's green and pleasant land.

Consumed by their own grief, nobody else had noticed that Marlo was breathing heavily, obviously struggling to contain a howl the likes of which that church hadn't heard in a long time. I looked up at Birdie, urging her to do something. She glanced at Marlo, then leaned across to me with a look of concern.

"I think she could do with some air, don't you?"

I nodded. Together, we led Marlo out the side door and sat her down on the stone wall by the entrance.

"You OK, sweetie?"

A tear rolled glumly down Marlo's flushed cheek, tapering at her chin before dripping heavily to the ground. It was the only one she allowed herself all day.

"It will get better. This is the worst day, I promise."

Nearby, voices were rising to an angry babble. Birdie craned her neck around the side of the building.

"Now what do you suppose all that's about?" she huffed. "Don't they know there's a funeral going on?"

I stood up.

"'Attaboy, Dominic!" Birdie stormed. "You go and tell those folks to show a little respect."

She didn't stop to consider what a ridiculous suggestion it was – her attention had already returned to Marlo. Curious, I peeled away nevertheless.

A crowd had gathered around the church notice board, where not one, but two pieces of paper now fluttered in the breeze. Both were covered in signatures.

"Looking for trouble, are you?" jeered a male voice. I swung around, but he wasn't talking to me. The man, a heavyset fellow in overalls and a squashed cap, was sniggering loudly at someone across the road.

Sancha.

"Go back to where you came from!" screeched a woman in a sun bonnet. She waved angrily at the Gypsy girl as if chasing off a vermin pest. "Go on – scat!"

Sancha didn't move. She had seen me.

"Come back to pinch some more booze for those layabout men of yours, eh?" bawled another man, hooking both thumbs through his suspenders. From where I stood, I could see that his thinning hair had been coaxed into an unconvincing side-sweep, creating an effect not dissimilar to that of a balding doll that Marlo had inherited from our grandmother. Wispy strands affixed to the doll's fabric scalp had always reminded me of a mummy I'd once seen at the British Museum, with its bits of ancient hair springing from the desiccated head. Here, now, I felt the same revulsion, watching the man in the suspenders swagger toward my friend.

"Why don't you make yourself scarce, you wretched creature?" shouted a young woman clutching a baby. "Honest people are trying to worship here!"

Still, Sancha did not move. Boots planted square, hands on hips, it was as if she was daring them to fight.

Ignoring the protests from the crowd, I slowly made my way to the knoll where she stood. *What are you doing here?* I wanted to hiss. *You're asking for trouble, and you know it!*

Sancha greeted me with cool eyes. "Stop," she said, when I was just a few feet away. I ground to a halt.

Excuse me?

"You've been with the *mulo?* The dead man?" she asked.

He has a name, you know. I nodded.

"I can't see you for a while, then," she said. "It's unclean."

Unclean? You came all this way to tell me that I'm unclean? You risked your family's safety by stirring up this stupid mob, just to tell me I'm unclean?

Sancha jerked her chin at the hecklers.

"Someone broke one of our windows last night. Threw this straight into our wagon – see?" and she pulled a piece of shale from her pocket, weighing it heavily in one hand. "It almost hit my mother while she was asleep."

I stared at the rock, struggling to absorb the meanness of its sharp angles and scars.

"They let the horses out, too. Took us until dawn to

get them all back and settle them down."

I nodded grimly. *I'm sorry.*

Sancha shoved the rock back into her pocket and glared over my shoulder at the crowd.

"Get away from her!" one of the women was shouting at me. "Run along home, boy. It's not for you to get involved with those scoundrels! They'll be kicked off that land soon enough, God willing."

Sancha spat at the ground.

"Stupid gadje," she muttered. The sun shone in her eyes, making the hazel flecks gleam like kelp floating in a deep sea. She let her arms flop to her sides and looked at me again. Her gaze softened, but only slightly.

"I wanted to say that I'm sorry he died."

Really?

"He hated it when the little ones begged," she said. "He was rude to them. But I wouldn't like it, either. I don't think he was bad." She shrugged. "Your sister liked him?"

I nodded again, and Sancha sighed. "I should go," she said.

By the time I returned to the church, the crowd had fallen still. Some of the women twittered dismissively; the men grumbled among themselves, eyeing me with a mixture of amusement and disdain. They were trying to judge me with their silence. Let them. I stuck my chin out as rudely as I thought fit, and cut a proud line through the group now hissing with whispers. Let them whisper.

When I found Birdie and Marlo again, my sister had

calmed down a little, and Birdie was fluttering with excitement. "What happened?" she begged. "You shut them up, all right!"

I fixed her with a determined stare, and wound up all the courage I could muster.

"Birdie," I said. "I need you to help me find something."

FIFTEEN

She took some convincing.

I suppose she was so taken aback by the fact that I'd finally spoken, she didn't really register what it was I was trying to say. When she finally did, she refused outright.

"No," she said. "Not on your life. It's not for kids, what I do. The last séance I did turned ugly. You'd expect a fellow who'd been brained with a tin of Tate & Lyle's treacle to turn sweet in the afterlife, but oh no – "

"Please, Birdie," I'd whispered breathlessly, almost wheezing in my effort to get the words out. I was terrified that we might be interrupted by some nosy passer-by. "You're the only one who can help me now. He didn't . . . he didn't give me anything else to go on – "

"No is *no*, Dominic!" she replied adamantly, sounding like a proper adult for the very first time. I must have looked pretty hurt, because she immediately began to rummage through her purse to avoid looking at me. "Anyway, even if we *were* going to ask the Reverend – which we most definitely are *not* – it would be far too soon to even think about contacting him now." She must have detected a glimmer of hope from me. "But I'm not even going to consider that as a possibility. *No.*"

And for about a week, I let her think that was it.

The following Sunday, when Auntie Sylv and Uncle Roo had gone to the farmers' market and Otto was busy writing, I brought the green book downstairs to show Birdie.

"He told me – " I tripped over my words, feeling as clumsy as Sancha's knock-kneed lamb. "He said that Lawrence had buried something. The Reverend spent years looking for it. He said it was a gift. Perhaps it was something from Prince Feisal – a sword, for instance. Or treasure . . ."

"Perhaps . . ." smiled Birdie.

I tried to ignore her amused expression. "Anyway, he mentioned that land . . . the land that's going to be sold. The Gypsy land, which the council wants to take away. Whatever it is that's buried there, it's not safe!" I struggled to process the words, lining them out in my head before speaking. Talking like this, to Birdie, was a new and exhausting experience. I gazed at her pleadingly. "He told me himself – Marlo was there – " and I glared at my sister, who nodded nervously.

Birdie toyed with the oversized beads draped loosely

down to her waist. She was lying on the fainting couch
in the sitting room with her feet on the armrest, staring
intently at the ceiling. Marlo was curled up on the overstuffed sofa, while I paced nervously up and down
the room.

"The Reverend had been looking for it ever since
Lawrence died," I said. Birdie nodded thoughtfully.

"So that explains his long walks across the moors,"
she muttered, more to herself than to me.

"He was about to find it. He was going to tell me
where, Birdie – I know he was. We just ran out of time."
I stopped pacing, trying to catch my breath. "He won't
rest until I've done what he told me to do. He doesn't
want it to just . . . to just stay wherever it is. He won't rest
until it's safe!"

Marlo whimpered nervously.

"Don't you fret, sugarpie," hushed Birdie soothingly.
"I'm sure he's resting just fine."

"But Birdie," I insisted, "think how . . . I mean, *think*
how important this could be. It's . . . it could be *valuable*."

Birdie shrugged.

"And who's to say he would want anyone digging it
up – whatever 'it' is?" she asked. "This fellow, from what
you're telling me, wanted to be left alone. After the war,
he only wanted to lead a normal life. He probably
wanted to forget some of it."

"*Normal?*" I shook my head. "You hate that word!"

She gazed at me with wide violet eyes. "If you'd been
Lawrence of Arabia, maybe you'd want a little normal,

too." After a thoughtful silence, Birdie heaved herself up to a sitting position. "That's not to say I wouldn't mind giving old Cleary a little shaking up on the other side," she smiled, with a mischievous glint.

"What do you mean?" frowned Marlo.

"Nothing sinister, sweetie," smiled Birdie. "But who am I to stand in the way of an old man's dying wish?"

"Do you think he's lonely . . . *over there?*" whispered my sister. I leapt at the opportunity to get her on side.

"You bet he is!" I said. "He'd be so thrilled – to – to know that we still cared enough – "

"Now really," groaned Birdie. "That old grump?"

"I think it might be nice," said Marlo, testing out the idea. "I mean, if you don't think we'd be disturbing him. He does like to talk sometimes, you know."

"Is that so, young lady?"

Marlo nodded tentatively, warming to the thought. "Oh, yes! He especially likes talking about pies."

"Sounds like a séance to me!"

Otto burst into the room with a clumsy soft-shoe shuffle. Immediately, Birdie turned defensive.

"Have you been eavesdropping all this time?" she barked.

"Me? Me!" cried Otto. He grinned broadly at me. "So what's the score, Dominic?"

I pursed my lips tightly.

"Well done, Otto," sighed Birdie. "Just as we were making some progress."

"Oh, come now," begged the jolly man, dropping like

a beach ball with limbs into the nearest armchair. "I've never experienced one of your famous séances, Birdie!"

"Nor are you going to," huffed Birdie, drawing herself upright. "There's not going to be a séance. It wouldn't be right."

But Birdie! I tried to plead with my eyes.

"Wouldn't, couldn't, shouldn't . . ." Otto groaned. "Those words don't mean anything to me. *Ban the conditional tense,* that's my motto!"

"There's another thing," said Birdie, crankily. "Their aunt and uncle would lynch me if they found out."

"Their aunt and uncle won't be in tonight," sang Otto. He beamed proudly at us. "They'll be at the planning meeting for the Larkspur Festival. Seven o'clock in the church hall!"

We all stared at him.

"Well, what's the problem, then? We're responsible adults – eh, Birdie? The kids will be well looked after." Otto wriggled in his seat and smacked his palms together. "What fun! Talk about excellent material for *Maxx Moriarty. . . .*"

"I don't know, Otto. . . ." Birdie shook her head. "The little one's been under a lot of strain already." She held up both hands, "No, no, no. Anyway, it's best to have groups in a number divisible by three. We'd be too many."

"What? Now you're just making things up!"

"I am *not!*"

"Birdie, *please,*" I interrupted. "It's not just about me, or the Reverend. It might help someone else. But I'll never know unless we find whatever it was the Reverend was looking for. He can't tell me where it is now – unless you help us."

"Hark at the boy!"

"It's serious," I snapped, and Otto instantly recoiled. "What good is a sixth sense if you don't use it?" I asked Birdie. "Come to think of it, what good have any of you ever done? Otto writes books that no one takes seriously; the Reverend composed music that no one understood. You're a group of has-beens and would-bes, and now you've got a chance to be something more. Wouldn't you like that, Birdie? To be more than just a mad lady who draws spooky pictures?"

Everyone was silent.

"My books aren't meant to be taken seriously," Otto mused. His voice was soft and tinged with reproach; he wasn't looking at me. "They're meant to be entertaining, that's all. I know that I'm no James Joyce."

It was as if someone had taken hold of my stomach and twisted it into a butterfly knot.

"I'm sorry, Otto," I said, feeling the heat rise to my skin. "I didn't mean it – "

"Of course you did!" Birdie's eyes were bright as she turned on Otto. "And he's right, too. The three of us were only ever going to be a bunch of failures – rejects, losers! Otherwise what were we doing all the way out here, at the end of the world? Hiding from our inadequacy, that's what." She began plumping the cushion behind her agitatedly. "Well, the kid's got a point."

"So you'll do it?" I tried not to sound too hopeful.

"You haven't left me any choice, have you, kiddo?" It was all I could do not to fling my arms around her then and there. "But only if you promise to let me do all the talking when we start. No jumping in until I say so, hear me?" Birdie bit her lip and smiled at me ruefully. "I'll tell you one thing, Dominic: you were a darn sight easier to handle when you didn't talk."

As soon as Uncle Roo and Auntie Sylv were out the door, we scampered upstairs like a gang of giddy children. Birdie made Otto bring Marlo's round dressing table into the Reverend's old room, and we each brought a chair to place around it.

"A medium can't recall most of what happens under a trance," explained Birdie, lighting a fat white candle that she placed with ceremonious care at the center of the table. "So you all will have to pay attention."

"Can do!" chirped Otto.

"What's the candle for?" asked Marlo.

"Protection," said Birdie, lowering the other lamps.

"Protection from what?"

"Never you mind."

Marlo eyed me anxiously. I don't know if she was too exhausted to get properly frightened, or too scared to go to bed. Either way, she was going to be included.

Birdie placed several sheets of blank paper and a pencil on the table.

"Now, once I've called him up, I'm going to start doing some automatic writing. I won't be able to read what it says, or even think about it until the séance is finished. So Dominic is going to ask all the questions he needs to." She shot a warning glance at Otto. "No interruptions. Only one person can talk at a time. And no jokes – spirits don't have much of a sense of humor once they've passed over."

We nodded in agreement. The curtains had been drawn; a thin strip of light slid under the door, and the candle flickered weakly on the table. Outside, a wind was building.

"We begin by laying our hands on the table," instructed Birdie. "Flat. Just touching the little finger of the person next to you." She was sitting between me and Otto. "You two will have to stretch across me. Keep the circle connected at all times."

She began to hum a low note, sustaining a long, even breath for well over a minute before addressing us, this time in a whisper. "I'd ask you all to close your eyes. Empty your minds."

That was rather difficult, considering all the questions swarming in my head. What to ask him first?

Several minutes passed. I began to wonder if I was falling asleep. Marlo and Otto made no sound.

"You can all open your eyes now. Keep your minds empty, and stay as still as you can."

Despite myself, I caught Otto's gaze. He winked at me.

"Peaceful spirit, we hope that you have found solace and quietude after your journey to eternal rest. We ask that the spirit of Reverend Cleary move among us tonight." Birdie's eyes were closed, her head tilted back just slightly. "Reverend Cleary, are you there?"

Silence.

"We invite you in peace. We ask that you will join us. There is someone here who wishes to fulfill a request you made. He needs your help now."

Marlo shifted uncomfortably. The candle flickered.

"Reverend Cleary, please: rap once on this table if you're here."

She had taken the pencil in one hand; the other steadied the paper before her. "Can you hear us? Please rap once if you are here. That's all we need."

At once, something landed with a thud below the table.

Startled, Marlo let out a tiny yelp. Otto's eyebrows almost shot off his head. I squinted down at the floor, feeling for whatever it was with my feet. Nothing.

"Was that you, Reverend Cleary?"

Marlo was staring at Birdie with wide eyes, mouth agape. The clairvoyant's hand had begun to move.

"Dominic would like to ask you some questions, Reverend. Take my hand; write through me as you will."

Another thud. Outside, a branch clattered against the windows like a hundred tapping fingers.

Otto nudged me with his toe; he, too, was searching for whatever it was that kept thumping beneath the table. Still, nothing.

Birdie's hand had begun to spiral across the page, forming a pattern like a cyclone.

Then words.

Ho

g

Was

Otto was frowning in disbelief.

"He's mocking us!"

"What?"

"Look!"

Hog

wash

I couldn't help smiling. It was the Reverend, all right.

"Dominic will ask you the first question."

I felt my heart begin to pound through my chest, pumping hollow, gushing noises between my ears. I pressed my hands into the table, steadying myself.

"Reverend Cleary?" I whispered. "It's me. You told me about something that Lawrence left behind when he was in Cornwall. He buried something, you said. And you were looking for it; you realized that you knew where it might be. But I don't know what it is, or where, or why you want me to find it – "

Otto inclined his head toward me. *Take it easy,* he seemed to say. *One at a time.*

I inhaled deeply.

"Reverend Cleary, was it a gift from Prince Feisal? A weapon, perhaps? The revolver you mentioned?"

Nothing.

"If it was a gift, who gave it to Lawrence? Do you know that?"

S

A

"Who's SA?" whispered Otto. I shrugged, helpless. Then it hit me.

"Selim Ahmed!" I cried. "That was Dahoum's real name . . ." Steadying myself, I asked, "Was it Dahoum, Reverend? Lawrence's friend, Dahoum?"

Before any more words could appear, Marlo began to giggle. Fierce with nerves, I shot her an impatient look.

"Stop it!" she squealed, grinning helplessly.

"Marlo?"

"Something's tickling me!" she gurgled breathlessly. After a moment, her giggles subsided. She glanced around, her smile evaporating. "It's stopped now," she said.

I exhaled slowly.

"Why did you want to find it, Reverend? It wasn't yours, after all. Maybe Lawrence didn't want it to be dug up."

More circles – but before any words appeared, a furious crash behind Otto brought us to a standstill. Three rows of books were swept from the shelf in the corner, tumbling to the floor in cascades of fluttering pages and flapping covers.

"You've upset him!" hissed Otto.

I tried not to panic.

"I'm sorry, Reverend Cleary," I hurried. "I didn't mean to offend you. It's just – I don't understand . . ."

Silence.

"I think he's gone," breathed Otto.

I shook my head. Birdie's pencil was still circling.

"Where is it?" I demanded from the shadows.

More words this time. Otto had to crane his neck to read Birdie's writing.

"*As . . . th . . .*" Otto sounded out the words as they formed. "*Crow* – I bet it's – yes! As the crow flies." He beamed in wonderment. "This is brilliant!"

"But how far, as the crow flies?" I asked again.

A long silence.

Squot.

"Squot?"

I read it again. "Where's Squot?" I asked.

Zsquot.

"It's nonsense," gasped Otto, as flummoxed as the rest of us.

Zrquit. Quoit. Zerquot.

"Perhaps he can't spell it," whispered Marlo.

Zrquoit.

"That's the second time he's written 'quoit,'" suggested Otto, trying to sound authoritative.

"Let's try something different," I said, impatient lest we lose the Reverend before I'd had a chance to ask all my questions. But before I could speak again, Birdie had started to write something else.

lone

ti

tiger

"Lone tiger," read Otto.

"What does it mean?" whispered Marlo. As if I should know.

But I did.

"The lone tiger," I said, slowly. "The lone Turkish tiger – Medina."

"What's that?"

"It's where the prophet Mohammed is buried. It's a sacred place. Lawrence waited to take Medina last. He let the Turks feel safe until the last minute, so they'd think that Medina was theirs. It was his final conquest. It's where the revolt ended."

Marlo gasped: "Medina Hill!"

I nodded.

"That's why you came here, isn't it, Reverend?" I swallowed hard. "Maybe, you knew you were going to die? After Annie passed away?"

Otto sighed heavily. "Christ on a cake . . ." he muttered.

At once, the candle extinguished.

"Now look what you've done!" squeaked Marlo.

"Sh!"

"Let him finish – "

Pb 8

7pilrd

hou

"The seven-pillared house . . ."

"Is that code for something?" asked Otto excitedly.

I shook my head. "I think Lawrence mentioned it in a message to Dahoum. . . . I don't know what it means."

Outside, the wind had ceased. Suddenly, the air felt very still. For the first time, I realised that I had been cold. Now, the temperature in the room was beginning to return to normal.

"Birdie?" I whispered. "Birdie, I think he's gone."

"Go in peace," incanted Birdie. "Thank you, friendly spirit. We shall leave you now. Go in peace."

Slowly, her hand ceased circling over the remaining sheet of paper. At the bottom was a cross.

Or a sword.

SIXTEEN

For several days, none of us spoke about what happened that night. Otto didn't want to discuss what words couldn't explain, and Birdie claimed that she couldn't remember anything. Whoever it was that had written those strange things through her, he hadn't given us nearly enough to go on. And that was assuming that whoever it was had actually been a real spirit.

Still, I didn't much fancy the thought of being haunted by a ghost with unfinished business for the rest of my life. And curiosity was getting the better of me.

One afternoon later that week, I found myself alone with Uncle Roo. He was cleaning out the Baron's coop at the end of the garden – a proper little house, with two floors and a miniature ladder and hoops and swings to play with. The Baron was perched on the uppermost peg, puffing his buff-pink breast feathers and blinking impatiently as we clumsily intruded on his privacy.

"Uncle Roo," I began, passing him a bag full of sawdust, "What's a . . . a quoit?" It came out sounding like *coyte*.

Uncle Roo sneezed loudly, banging his head on the inside of the coop.

"Blast!"

"Uncle Roo?"

"What's that, son?" He furrowed his brow as he spread clean sawdust evenly about the bottom floor. "Do you mean a *kwayte?*"

I shrugged. "I don't know how you say it. It was written on . . . in . . . in a book."

Uncle Roo straightened himself, brushing his hands.

"Reading about the pagans and the ancients now, are you? Moved on from Arabia?"

I attempted a confident grin, shoving my hands in my pockets with the kind of swagger the tough boys got away with back home. "Oh yes, Uncle Roo. I got tired of Arabia. I'm all read up on the ancients now."

I hated to have to lie through my teeth, but Uncle Roo didn't seem to think anything of it.

"A quoit, dear boy, is a stone tomb. Different from the *fogous,* which are underground caves dating back to the Iron Age. There's a few around here that were used as Royalist hiding places during the Civil War . . ." He stopped himself. "I digress. It's quoits you're after, eh?" I nodded. "This part of the country is full of them – hundreds, maybe even thousands of years old. Of course, they might have been cenotaphs, rather than actual mausoleums." He scratched his head thoughtfully. "Funny old things. Some have collapsed – you have to be careful."

As far as I knew, tombs belonged in cemeteries. I didn't fancy a trip to the church, with all those angry people likely to be milling about.

Uncle Roo gazed out to sea with a nostalgic air. "In fact, I used them as practice for the Baron during the war. Started with Zennor Quoit when he was a few months old, then moved farther out – Lanyon Quoit, Chun Quoit, Mulfra Quoit. We tested his homing instinct from all over the county."

Zrquoit – Zennor Quoit?

"Isolated things, strewn about the moor like a giant game of jacks. Except most of the stones are flat slabs – not boulders really. They were chiselled a long time ago."

My mind raced. *Sancha's fort.* "Could the Baron still find his way home, do you think?"

"Could he!" Uncle Roo laughed. "He found his way all over France, remember – and that, with mortar blasts and shrapnel, and airplanes whizzing about overhead!" He chuckled proudly. "Getting back from the quoits would be a doddle for the old Baron."

This was too good to be true. "Uncle Roo, do you suppose I could take the Baron out with me today?"

"Around the moors, you mean?"

"Not far . . ."

Uncle Roo scratched his head again and sighed heavily. "It's not the Baron I worry about, Dominic – it's you. I don't want you running into trouble out there all alone. Especially with the Romany problems we've been having. . . ."

"*Please*, Uncle Roo?" I took a deep breath. "I promise I'll keep to the paths."

Uncle Roo grinned, ruffling my hair.

"All right," he agreed, after a pause. "If you promise."

He reached into the upper level of the coop and pulled out a smooth white feather.

"Used to find a lot of these, during the war," he muttered, with a wry smile.

"Oh?"

He passed the feather to me. It felt soft between my fingers. "For those of us who didn't join up. The white feathers were sent around as a kind of . . ." he searched for the right word. "Accusation. Of cowardice."

I considered the delicate fringe of fine white barbs uniting in a perfect wave. Uncle Roo shrugged. "It always seemed a shame to make a mockery of something so lovely."

I nodded in agreement. My uncle straightened. "Here," he said, in a different voice, tossing me a leather glove from the coop. "You put this on, and let the Baron perch on your wrist – " As he whistled, the bird fluttered down to my hand, "like that. You know how I trained him, don't you?" I shook my head. "The old-fashioned way: holding him on my arm for two whole days and nights, waiting for him to fall asleep."

"But why?"

"That's how long it took him to trust me. Now he sees the glove as a safe place; whoever wears it is his master." The pigeon was stronger than he appeared, and he weighed heavily on my arm, tiny talons clinching at the hardy glove.

Next, Uncle Roo picked up a small red pouch that rattled temptingly, and put it in my other hand. "These are his Christmas treats. Only to be used in an emergency." The Baron began to puff his feathers in excitement. "He goes wild for them. Works better than a lead!"

"I'll take good care of him, Uncle Roo."

"Be back for tea, mind. Your sister wants to test out those cream swirls on us, remember?"

I grinned. The poor kid was working herself into a right tizz over that competition.

The sky was a hazy blue veil that afternoon, shimmering with the promise of a storm. Breathing through the muggy atmosphere was like trying to extract air from a damp dishcloth. Suffocated by the humidity of the valley, I looked forward to striking out onto the windswept moor once again. Getting there should be easy enough. Getting back might be harder: with Sancha, we'd returned at dusk, and I didn't trust my memory. A homing pigeon would come in handy should I lose my way.

The moor was as I remembered it; barren green-gray land, sparsely patched with hardy wildflowers. Trudging across the rugged ground was hard work, and I reminded myself, rather sheepishly, that I was still no country boy.

As I walked, my thoughts wandered to Sancha and the kumpania. How many times had she followed this same route, with only distant birdsong for company and a great blue canopy of sky overhead? I'd always thought of Gypsies as free; wanderers who never had to observe the rigid boundaries and dull rules that I'd learned to tolerate. But Sancha couldn't always have felt free – not with neighbors who attacked her family's home. Not with a wooden leg that made her an outsider among the other children.

I scowled into the wind. Maybe this was my chance to do something. Lawrence had traveled hundreds of miles to find friends in Prince Feisal and Dahoum. When he saw what was happening in Arabia, he poured all his energy into helping them.

My thoughts gathered speed. I could tear up that rotten petition for starters. I could build a barricade around the Gypsy camp, so no one could get in to release the horses again. I could even break a few village windows in the dead of night, and see how they'd like it–

And then, it appeared: an exposed pile of rocks clustered together, sheltering against the surrounding emptiness. I quickened my pace, heart catching a beat.

Bedouin gravesites are recognized for their simplicity, began one chapter in the green book. It described the funeral

of a warrior that Lawrence had come to know during
the revolt.

> Funeral guests add stones to the burial mound: one
> near the head of the deceased person, and one at
> the foot. Sometimes, they attach written expressions
> of grief. In an ancient Arab custom, the mount of
> the dead warrior is tied to the tomb and left to die
> by its master's side.

I stood before the quoit and tried to rid my thoughts
of graves and funerals. Uncle Roo had said that the
quoits weren't actual burial chambers. *It's not a grave,* I
told myself. *It's only a cenotaph, like the monument for soldiers
who died in the war.*

Baron Sigwalt seemed happy to perch on the capstone while I went inside to investigate. Against my
uncle's instructions, I spread out a few of his Christmas
treats to keep the old pigeon satisfied.

Why had I not noticed it before? The mound of earth
piled up against the back wall – it was comparatively
fresh, bare of moss or weedy overgrowth. I dropped to
my knees and pulled out a small trowel that I'd hidden
in one pocket. I began to dig.

The soil was damp and sweet-smelling; I had to work
quite hard to break through dense lumps that had
cooled into bricks, shifting the pile inch by inch with
painstaking care.

I dug for a very long time. I don't know why I had

expected it to be easy. It wasn't. Once or twice I poked
my head out to make sure that the Baron was still there;
he was, but the Christmas treats were gone. I scattered
a few more and returned to work.

Just as I was about to give up, the trowel jammed
against something. I tested the ground again and felt
resistance – a promising sign. Several minutes later, and
there it was. I brushed off the remaining flecks of dirt,
suddenly weak with anticipation.

I had discovered a biscuit tin.

The lid was decorated with a picture of a country
kitchen and emblazoned with the words *All Butter
Shortbread* in swirling gold letters. Something inside made
a gentle *thunk* as I dislodged the box from the ground,
and I swallowed hard.

At first I tried to pry the lid open with my fingernail,
but it wouldn't budge. I cast around for something sharp
and flat, and quickly reached for a piece of flint jutting
out of the pile of upturned soil. I slid the pointed end
under the lid and gently levered one corner out. With a
sudden *pop!* the lid swung open.

Whatever was inside had been wrapped in stiff oil-
cloth. I carefully drew back the corners of the bundle,
growing increasingly impatient as each new layer
revealed fresh folds. Until suddenly, peeking out from
the depths, something caught my eye.

It was a terra-cotta statue, pink, and no taller than
a gravy boat: a rider astride his horse. The animal's legs
were short, its tail a knotted stump, its bridle cleverly

wound with hardened clay. The rider's features were strangely naïve: two wide eyes and a hawked nose emerged from beneath a pointed helmet. His legs had been forged into the horse's body so that they appeared as one, and his hands melted into the horse's brushy mane. The figurine had been carved out of rough, baked clay, and though it looked like stone, it was very light.

If what the Reverend had said was true – if Dahoum had given this to Lawrence – it would have been when they last saw each other, at the archaeological dig. Lawrence must have buried it here after learning that Dahoum had died. The quoit had become its final resting place.

I studied the figurine closely, allowing my thoughts to tumble into place. Lawrence and Dahoum had discovered jewelry, weapons, bronze, and pottery at Deve Huyuk; this might well have been one of the objects unearthed at a military gravesite. Which would make it a Persian horse, and old – very old. Some of the things Lawrence unearthed dated from the eighth century BC. And here it was now, in my hands.

Something happened in that moment that is hard to describe. Lawrence, who for so long had existed only in my imagnation, suddenly became real. If the Reverend was to be believed, I was the first person to hold this little statue since the man who discovered it. His fingers must have run over the same brittle surface, traced the outline of the horse's bridle and the rider's peaked helmet, and marveled at the surprising lightness of the figurine. This was as real as Lawrence would ever be, even more alive to me now than in the book.

I raised the statue against the gray light. It really was very small. And yet I couldn't help but admire this brave little horseman, whoever he was, riding valiantly out of the past into a strange, new world. He had come from a land of cypress trees and sand dunes, crescent moons and dancing girls and goatskin tents and smoking hookahs, and somehow he had ended up here, in soggy England. The war had done this to him. The war hung over the little horseman just as it hung over Dad and Uncle Roo.

I felt as if I should say something to mark this occasion, as a sign of respect. The only Arabic I knew was from the green book: the very first greeting that Lawrence had learned when he first arrived in the Middle East, meaning "peace be upon you."

"*As Salâm 'alekum,*" I whispered.

The rain came suddenly.

Outside, the Baron was flapping irritably and making near-human grumbling sounds. Two of his Christmas treats remained on the capstone, but they had quickly turned soggy and he wasn't interested in nibbling at defective goods. The miserable little fellow blinked at me impatiently, as if to say "May we go now, if Master has completed his business?"

"Come on, Baron," I sighed, emerging from the

quoit with the biscuit tin in one hand. I was reluctant to allow the figurine to get wet, but I couldn't bear to leave it, either. "Home!"

He fluttered on ahead, wings billowing on the gusting wind, occasionally returning to circle me as if to check my progress and hurry me on. Dark clouds banked on the horizon, rolling low. The rain had started pouring down in heavy sheets, and at times I lost sight of him completely through the dazzling storm.

Within seconds, I was soaked through, exhausted from the hard shoveling, trembling with cold and excitement – and maybe a little fear. Had it really been such a good idea to remove the horseman from his resting place? If I was found out, would I be accused of theft? Would Lawrence himself come to wreak his revenge, resplendent in flowing robes, wielding a flashing sabre?

I was dreaming again – a waking dream.

When next I looked around, the Baron had disappeared from sight. A thick mist was rising across the horizon, like a company of spirits seeping from the ground. I shivered, hugging the tin to my chest. Which way was I supposed to be going?

With a sinking feeling, I realized that I could no longer tell one end of the moor from the other; I could barely make out my own hand, let alone the distant cliffs. The wind shrieked through streams of rain, sending a swelling rumor of sound across the empty landscape. Water pounded relentlessly down from a blackening sky, rolling in heavy gusts that almost swept my feet from under me. Battered from all angles, I finally collapsed to the ground, desperate to feel something still and firm and unyielding.

How had this happened? Where was I?

After several minutes, a sharp whistle brought me to my senses. Shielding my face from the bulleting raindrops, I squinted into the sky. I had just made out a flash of white collar feathers when the Baron disappeared from view again. Moments later, he had returned. He swooped upon me, nicking the back of my head with his tiny talons, before veering off to one side. I picked myself up, and began fighting my way after him.

Somehow I got home; I don't know if it took minutes or hours. After a swift inspection to confirm that I recognized the house — clearly, he didn't think much of my own homing instincts — the Baron fluttered into his coop, nestling cozily in the warm, dry straw without giving me a second glance. His job was done.

After tossing him the last of the treats, I hurried straight to my room — ignoring Marlo's exclamation of surprise as I squelched through the kitchen, a wretched, sodden mess — and shoved the tin under my bed.

It had waited long enough already. It could wait a little longer.

SEVENTEEN

Birdie might have been the one with mystical powers, but Otto had a nose for secrets. He knew something was up straight away.

"So, what news from the Arabian front?" he asked, slyly.

We had just finished dinner, and I was curled up by the fireplace in the sitting room, notepad and pencil in hand. Birdie and Auntie Sylv were helping Marlo clear the kitchen from a day of cream swirls, honey cake, and fig tarts. Despite her efforts so far, my sister had yet to decide on her entry for the baking competition. The festival was only a few days away.

Glimpsing Uncle Roo out of the corner of my eye, I pretended to scribble something on my notepad. I didn't want to tell anyone about the terra-cotta horseman — not yet, anyway. What I had found was special: a fragile line connecting me to a real hero. Without meaning any harm, Otto would break the delicate bond like a bear crashing through a spider's web. Now that the horseman was in my care, it was my responsibility to protect it – and that meant keeping it a secret, for the time being, at least.

"Oh, for the imagination of youth! My own inspiration has vanished. All I managed to muster today was tripe, pure tripe – vanity! Cliché! Pompous rambling!" he grimaced comically. "If only I had a tale worth telling. A tale of . . ." he shot me a twinkling glance, "unlikely heroes? Hidden treasures . . ." he nodded knowingly at my notepad, slowing down. "Revolt? . . . in the *desert?*"

"You're too late, Otto," laughed Uncle Roo from behind his papers. "The boy's gone off Arabia."

"Wouldn't bet on it," smiled Otto. "You know, Dominic," he said to me, "a rumor went round earlier this year that Lawrence's death had been faked by the secret service so he could carry out special operations overseas *incognito.*"

"Otto, the boy's not interested – " sighed Uncle Roo.

"But look at this!" and Otto jerked his thumb at the notepad, peering over my shoulder. "*The seven-pillared house . . .*"

It was one of the things I'd copied down from the séance.

"Tackling *The Seven Pillars of Wisdom,* are you?" said Uncle Roo, looking vaguely impressed. "Lawrence's masterpiece. Not exactly a light read."

What does it mean? I wrote. I looked up to Otto, hopeful. Speaking in front of him was still a struggle. His very presence seemed to squeeze out any space for my words.

"Biblical, isn't it?" snorted Otto. "The seven-pillared house?"

"From the Book of Proverbs, I think you'll find," smiled Uncle Roo, disappearing behind his paper once more.

Proverbs.

I frowned at my notes.

Pb8

I leapt to my feet and hurried swiftly upstairs.

Being in the Reverend's room wasn't as spooky as you might have expected, even though someone had died there. It felt calm peaceful, somehow.

There was a Bible on his desk. Grabbing it, I heaved myself onto the bed and began to flip nervously through the feather-thin pages.

Proverbs 8
Does not wisdom call out?
Does not understanding raise her voice?

Who was I to raise my voice? What wisdom? I skimmed through the passage that followed, struggling to make rhyme or reason of it.

Listen, for I have worthy things to say;
I open my lips to speak what is right.

My mouth speaks what is true,
for my lips detest wickedness.
All the words of my mouth are just;
none of them is crooked or perverse.

He wanted me to say something. But to whom? For what? And why me – a boy who didn't speak?

That was when I realized that the Reverend's notebook was missing from the desk. I'd only seen it once before – the night that Marlo and I had entered the room to kneel at his bedside – but I could still picture it clearly. I looked in the drawers, but all I found there were a pencil, some stamps and a ball of string.

For all I knew, the notebook was for his sermons – either that, or his musical compositions. But I knew what sheet music looks like, and I couldn't remember seeing any staves or clefs on those pages. Could the book have contained a record of his searches on the moors? The thought that all the answers I was looking for might be clearly written in one place was almost too much to bear.

I screwed my eyes shut and tried to picture Lawrence. Not the hero in the white robes, brandishing a jewel-encrusted sword; not the bloodied warrior, or the wise prophet. The solitary wanderer. Who, as a boy, had escaped his parents' shame by immersing himself in Arthurian legends and collecting brass rubbings of medieval tombs from local churches. He had been a misfit among his own people, and a curiosity to the Arabs. He must have known my loneliness.

I closed my eyes more tightly, gripping the Bible with both hands, and still all I could see were flashes of blue and white against the pink darkness of my eyelids. All I could hear were the same downstairs sounds: someone tuning the wireless, a burst of laughter from the kitchen, the clatter of dishes as Auntie Sylv took over the washing up.

I closed the Bible with a thump and retreated from the room.

No one raised an eyebrow when I went to bed early that night. Marlo was oblivious to me, consumed by her own anxiety about the competition. The grown-ups were subdued; no one suggested charades after dinner. Charades was one of my best games.

Once again, I unpacked the terra-cotta horseman from the tin. Turning it over in my hands, I wished that he could speak, to tell me what to do next. Lawrence was gone; so was the Reverend. And yet I couldn't keep the figure to myself forever. It wasn't mine to keep.

I must have fallen asleep, because I sat up with a jerk at a tapping noise at the window.

At first I put it down to tree branches brushing against the glass. But on this side of the house, none of the trees reached past the second floor. I returned the horseman to the biscuit tin and slid it under the bed. Then I stood up, bare feet tickled by the cool floorboards, and crept to the window.

A cluster of loose pebbles clattered against the glass, making me jump.

There she was, swaying nervously in the shadows, square face turned up with a look of impatient expectation. "*Dominic,*" she hissed. "Are you there?"

I heaved the creaking window open, and stuck my head out. *What are you doing here?* I wanted to whisper. *I thought you couldn't see me. You said I was unclean.*

As usual, Sancha didn't wait for a reply. "We're having a feast. Do you want to come?"

My mind raced. *Why? And how? Your family wouldn't like it—*

Sancha scowled. "We can be careful – I brought you a hat!" She pulled out a beaten cap from her back pocket. Some disguise.

I don't know Sancha . . .

"Are you coming or not, gadjo?" she barked.

I instantly raised a warning finger to my lips. *Keep it down!*

"Well?"

I glanced around the room for my shoes. *One minute,* I motioned.

We scurried down the darkening path together, my stomach twisting in excitement. Sancha may have had a game leg, but the girl could move. She led me by the hand through a shortcut in the woods, confidently brushing aside the outstretched limbs of trees and bracken. I stumbled and clambered along as clumsily as a bear, while she fled swiftly, almost soundlessly through the forest – as if she'd somehow memorized every last branch, every crevice, every gnarled root. Neither of us said a word, our shallow breathing the only sound in the deepening twilight.

At last, she landed with a thump behind an enormous log at the edge of the clearing. At first I thought she had tripped; then I noticed the lights and sounds of a gathering just twenty yards away. Sancha waved an impatient hand at me, urging me to crouch. I joined her on the ground, peering nervously over the top of the log at the scene before us.

They were dancing: a wild, joyful dance. Someone strummed heartily on a guitar, accompanied by the harmony of a couple of mouth-organs. The women waved their skirts in brash, sweeping movements, shrieking and laughing, gaily spinning circles around the men, who slapped their thighs and clapped and cheered raucously.

"The men will start showing off soon," said Sancha. In the half-light, her eyelashes cast spider shadows across her cheeks. "My dad will perform tricks with his whip – he can slice a carrot in half in one sweep."

Nearby, a bonfire blazed furiously, licking at a row of chickens turning on a blackened spit. Children raced through the darkness, banging on tambourines and blowing piercing nonsense through wooden flutes, tilting with pretend swords made from branches, and leaping like leprechauns around the glowing embers.

"You smell that?" asked Sancha, sniffing at the breeze. A musky, almost nutty scent slipped past my nose, stirring memories of bitter chocolate.

I nodded, intrigued.

"My mother is over there," She pointed to a graceful woman wearing a crimson shawl and a dove-gray skirt that trailed to the ground. Her black hair was plaited in loops, and as she stirred at the contents of a squat iron pot, a few loose curls teased her smooth forehead. Silver hoop earrings brushed gently against her slender neck. "She's beautiful," Sancha stated matter-of-factly. "My sister is more like my father – dark. Everyone says I am like my *dai,* my mother."

In that moment, I began to ache for my own mother, alone in a hospital ward. I still had not written her any of the letters I had promised.

"That's coffee you can smell – she makes it from roasted dandelion roots. You want some?"

Reluctantly, I shook my head. Dad said I wasn't allowed coffee until I was sixteen. He'd always made it sound like something you didn't take up until you were good and ready, unless you'd been brought up a bit rough. The same went for smoking.

Sancha shrugged.

"I'll get us some food," she whispered, pulling the cap roughly over my ears. "You stay here."

Before I could respond, she was gone.

By the time she returned, the dancing had given way to a melancholy tune. One man lightly plucked at the guitar while a woman sang. Sancha's mother was still stirring the pot, silver bangles clinking an irregular beat to the music. I imagined that they sounded like the metallic jingle of the fringed saddles used on Arabian horses – the sort of sound Lawrence would have grown used to in the desert. Transfixed by the haunting melody, I barely noticed Sancha return, hands full of sticky chicken pieces.

"Have some – it's good," she ordered.

It was. Smoky and sweet – maybe it had something to do with being cooked outside. We gobbled up what must have amounted to an entire chicken in minutes flat.

Sancha spat out a bone and wiped her hands brusquely on her shorts. "They're singing about *latcho drom*," she explained casually. "The long road our people have traveled. Over hundreds of years."

I nodded. "Latcho drom," I whispered.

The girl whipped around to stare at me, jaw dropping like a broken hinge. "You spoke!" she said, voice hushed and uncertain.

I felt myself go red. I hadn't planned to say anything. I certainly hadn't thought about the words. They just came out, like that: *latcho drom*.

"What else can you say, gadjo?" laughed Sancha, quickly recovering from her surprise. "Eh? You say other things, too?"

I frowned. I wasn't a toddler learning to speak. It

wasn't a trick. "I'd like to learn your language," I blurted, somewhat huffily.

Sancha's smile vanished.

"You can't," she replied. "Gadje can't speak Romani. You wouldn't understand it."

"But I just did!"

"That's only two words. And for those two words, we can come up with a hundred more," insisted Sancha proudly. "Our language is one thing the gadje can't take from us, see?"

The hot chicken crumpled painfully inside me. More words. More barriers. I rose to my feet, brushing myself off. "Then I'm going," I said. "Thanks for the food."

"But why—" She leapt up, trying to steady me with one hand.

"No," I insisted, shrugging her off more violently than I intended. "You can't just bring me here to watch your people, to . . . to eat your food – and then, when I ask . . . when I ask to learn your language, to throw it back at me like . . . like some stupid toy!" I struggled to control my breathing, my thoughts. "A stupid baby who can't share her toys!"

"Wait—" She looked genuinely concerned.

"I'm going," I repeated, hating myself even as the words tumbled out. "I'm going back – to *my* people." I'm ashamed to say it, but I left her there. Just like that.

And in the distance, the song trailed out note by note – until there was nothing.

EIGHTEEN

There were a few nights when I imagined that I heard the sound of pebbles clattering against my window. I never got up to investigate, though – simply rolled over and sank back into sleep. It was easier that way.

The day before the festival, Marlo summoned me to the kitchen for a Top Secret Meeting.

Everything was coated with flour – even my sister. Pots, pans, and mixing bowls were piled up in the sink; breadboards, whisks, rolling pins, and ladles were strewn across the counters; and on the refectory table, dozens of plates displayed a multitude of treats the likes of which I'd never seen before.

"Those are blackberry tarts, next to the fairy cakes . . . and those are coffee biscuits, with rosebud madelines. Those are just boring old blueberry muffins," explained Marlo, with surprising authority.

"And that?"

"What, the apricot flan? Or the butterscotch cake?"

"That one," I pointed.

"Chestnut galette. And chocolate loaf, lemon gateau, rhubarb crumble, spice cakes . . . treacle duff, tipsy cake . . . plum pudding, cinnamon buns . . ." Marlo raised a finger thoughtfully to her lips, frowning. "The gooseberry clafoutis doesn't look quite like the picture. Or the Madeira cake." She frowned.

"Is that a Victoria sponge?"

"Mm."

"What about that one, with the cream?"

"Peach cream pie. Or these? They're called profiteroles. That's rosemary shortbread."

"And trifle?

"Raspberry," nodded Marlo.

It was a truly majestic medley, each and every item turned out in its Sunday best.

"Blimey, Marlo – "

"Pick one!" she ordered.

"It looks brilliant . . . I can't believe you did all of this – "

"Pick one!" she repeated, voice rising shrilly. I turned to her, slightly taken aback. "What's wrong with you?"

"I can only enter *one* of these into the competition!"

I shrugged. "Well, you know I like chocolate . . ."

"The loaf isn't pretty enough, though. Even with icing sugar."

"Well, then . . ." I scanned the multitude of pastries,

pies, tarts, cakes, and biscuits. "The sponge looks nice."

"*Nice* isn't good enough to win, Dominic!" insisted Marlo. She shook her head ruefully. "Anyway, someone else will have made Victoria sponge. It's too . . . *obvious.*"

I sighed. "Look, you asked me what I thought . . ."

"The galette is fancy, but the peach pie is more . . . *summery.*"

"Right. So peach pie it is, then."

"No!"

"Marlo, calm down!"

Marlo hiccupped, eyes blurring with frustration. "I can't calm down," she moaned. "The Reverend said I had to win! I've tried every recipe in the book, plus a few from Auntie Sylv. But nothing seems right." She gestured vaguely at the table and flopped into a chair.

I frowned, desperate to help. And then it struck me. "What about the pies?"

"I've already told you – "

"No, I meant the Reverend's pies."

Marlo stared at me blankly. "The pork and apple ones?" she shook her head. "I don't have a recipe for those."

I tried not to laugh. "You're telling me you'd *need* a recipe? After all this?"

She contemplated the table. "I don't know," she said. "I could probably manage the pastry. . . ."

"Well, then. There's got to be one or two left in the icebox. You could compare with those."

"I'd never thought of using his pies," my sister

mumbled to herself. "They're not exactly puddings . . ."

"So? It's a baking competition, Marlo." I picked up *The New Art of Cooking,* no longer pristine and neat, but splattered with dried blobs of egg and flecks of batter. I closed it firmly. "You don't need to depend on the recipes anymore. You know enough now."

My sister pursed her lips and sniffed. As she rubbed her nose, a light dusting of flour streaked across her face. I smiled.

"What?"

"Nothing, nothing – I'll leave you to it."

Penwith's Larkspur Festival must have been the proudest day of the year for local folk. There were prizes on offer for the maddest things you can imagine, from giant vegetables to egg rolling. It was obvious that some people had been preparing for weeks, making home-made jams for the preserves stall, practicing for the dog show, and raising cattle and sheep for the livestock competition. A local band struck up jolly, old-fashioned tunes while candy floss materialized in spinning barrels and roly-poly bakers served up plates of scones smothered in Cornish clotted cream. All the ladies turned out in their best frocks and bonnets, while the gents clutched tankards of cider, and kids streamed through the gates looking like they'd arrived in heaven.

Before joining the other grown-ups at the honey stall, Uncle Roo had handed us a few shillings and told us to spend it wisely. It was hard to know where to begin – skittles or ring-the-bottle? Splat-the-rat or the sponge toss?

"What's that?" asked Marlo, pointing to a crowd of people queuing up in front of a tent decorated with streams of flashing lights. A painted sign beckoned: COCONUT SHY – tuppence for six tries!

"Come on," I said.

Inside the tent, six coconuts balanced precariously on wooden posts. Each person was given six wooden balls to try and knock off as many as they could. If you managed to topple them all, there was a fresh coconut for a prize. As we inched closer, a couple of lucky kids passed by sucking at straws, greedily slurping the fresh coconut juice. Marlo's eyes widened.

"Ooh, I'd like one of those," she cooed. The kid had perked right up after submitting her entry to the baking competition earlier that morning. I checked the board.

"It's tuppence a go," I said. "We'll both try it."

The man in charge handed me two balls, and I squared up to the first post, eyeing the hairy brown coconut perched on top. Just as I was winding up, someone bumped into me roughly from behind.

As my first ball dribbled pathetically short of the post, I spun around to catch the offender – a skinny kid in a prissy dress and straw hat. Her gaze met mine, her expression a veil of calm.

"Look where you're going, gadjo," hissed Sancha. She edged me to one side. "You throw like a girl."

"You pushed me!"

Sancha smirked. Apart from the black Wellingtons, her clothes had changed completely. It was strange to see her in a dress. For once, she looked – well, like a girl.

It's a disguise, I thought to myself. *She's trying to fit in.*

"Go on, then," she jeered. "I'll even let you have one of mine."

I missed the first toss. And the second. In fact, I missed all six. Marlo didn't do any better.

When Sancha threw her first toss, the ball sent that coconut spinning off its post as if it had been struck by a bullet. The second one split from the force of her throw. It was like watching cannon fire. When she was done, she turned to face me, smug.

"Let your sister have it," she said, passing me her prize. The coconut was heavier than it looked.

"Is that your Gypsy friend?" asked Marlo. I ignored her.

Sancha trailed us all day, winning at everything, while I kept losing. I'm not sure what my sister made of it, but she couldn't have been too bothered – every time Sancha won an ice lolly or a balloon or even a real live goldfish in its own glass bowl she handed the prize straight to Marlo. Sometimes she'd throw me a pitying glance before slouching off to the next game.

The final event was the tug-of-war. For this, at least, I couldn't blame myself if we lost. There were fifteen of us kids in all, so one team was going to have an extra person. As soon as the adults in charge had divided us up according to our size, Sancha made a beeline for the team that was going to be one child short. I could have sworn she shot me a sly grin as she took up the rope at the front of the line.

"Are you ready, everyone?" boomed a man in a wide-brimmed hat.

"Yes!" we shouted.

"Right-o! Three! Two! One! HEAVE!"

The rope chafed painfully after a few seconds, as I dug my feet stubbornly into the ground. The boy in front of me seemed to be leaning virtually horizontal, groaning with the strain of it, and we inched farther back. Then, a sharp tug from Sancha sent us lurching forward. This happened several times, and we struggled to make up the lost ground by pulling even harder at that rope, sliding into each other out of sheer desperation.

And then, the rope fell slack. Like a row of dominoes, we tumbled one upon the other with shocked grunts and squeals, hands burning, arms floppy as rubber.

"The winners!" proclaimed the man in the hat, and a fat woman in a floral dress wobbled forward to present each child on Sancha's team with a noisemaker prize.

A queue for hot food had begun to snake around the hog roast as the silent auction winners were announced. All day long, people had been adding their admission numbers to the prize lists in the hope that when the final bell rang, theirs would be the last – and highest – bid. One by one, the winners were called out for all sorts of prizes:

dinner for two at a local restaurant; gift certificates from a department store in Truro; flower arranging classes; horse-riding lessons; party catering; a ride in a hot air balloon; tickets to a cricket final . . . the list went on. Some people had bid a few shillings on the lesser prizes and won; one or two had spent many pounds in order to trump rival bids. I'd begun to wonder why we'd not bothered to enter, when the final item was announced.

"And last, but by no means least," rippled the presenter's voice through a tinny loudhailer, "we'll be announcing the winning bid for the most highly anticipated prize of the day."

An expectant hush swept the crowd. Families waiting to be served dinner, children lining up at hook-the-duck, gents drinking in the beer tent, little kids squirming out of their fancy-dress costumes, older lads circled around an impromptu wrestling match, ladies clustered in front of the high-roller tombola – for that moment, everyone's attention was focused on the annoncer.

"What is it?" whispered Marlo.

"Tonight, one lucky person will leave this festival the proud owner of . . ." the presenter, a spry little man in a yellow bow tie, was clearly enjoying the attention, "*twelve acres of arable pasture extending from Medina Hill to Trewhalley Wood!* Formerly the property of the local council, it has been decided by popular consensus that the land is to enter private hands."

As the crowd raised a cheer, I realized which bit of land he meant. The Romany site.

"And the winner of this . . . *ahem*—" the presenter stifled a mock cough, "—soon-to-be-vacated property . . ."

The crowd chuckled wryly.

He unfolded the paper with painful deliberation. "Is the holder of ticket number sixty-three, with a bid of *one hundred pounds!*"

I glanced around in disbelief. Surely they couldn't be doing this – selling off all that land, land where people had come to live every year for centuries, as part of a fairground spectacle?

"Would the person with ticket sixty-three please come forward! *Six-tee-three!*"

There was movement to one side of the stage. Someone was approaching the steps – a girl in a straw hat.

She thumped lopsidedly up to the platform, allowing herself a moment of composure before thrusting her ticket into the presenter's outstretched hand. Then, beaming, Sancha tossed her hat into the crowd. *"Romany!"* she cried.

After a split second of stunned silence, the audience erupted into storms of protest.

"Get down from there, you little hussy!" shouted a strawberry-nosed man.

"Check her ticket!" added another, eyes glittering.

"They can't afford the land, anyway!"

"Yes we can!" shouted Sancha. "Last year my father offered you people twice as much for it, but your council wouldn't accept our money!"

"Filthy Gyppo!" spat a man in horn-rimmed glasses.

"And we don't want it now, either!"

"Re-draw! Re-draw!" chanted others.

The announcer examined the ticket closely. He twiddled nervously with his tie before raising the loudhailer slowly to his lips.

"It's . . . the ticket is legitimate," he stuttered. "We can't refuse to honor a bid in a public auction. We would have to start all over again . . ." But his voice was drowned out by a hundred others.

"The land's already been reclaimed by the council – "

"The petition was voted on!"

"Tell the girl to scram!"

"And her parents, too!"

"Where's the money?"

"She'll have stolen it, and then it'll be too late – "

"Dirty knacker!"

Marlo tugged at my sleeve. "Dominic," she whispered anxiously, "Do something!"

I swallowed hard. Sancha's face was drawn and tired; she no longer managed even the faintest glimmer of a smile. Her eyes flashed, but I could tell by her drooping shoulders that she had no more strength.

"The bid was mine!" I hollered.

Silence – the dreaded, hollow sound of hope about to be dashed. I steeled myself against it and plowed through the crowd. Everything went quiet: a bit like the feeling you get after swimming under water, when your ears are blocked and temporary deafness sets in. An instant later, I found myself standing on the stage next to Sancha.

Amid the blur of faces, I managed to pick out Marlo's. My little sister was grinning from ear to ear, hands clasped nervously to her chest. Behind her, Uncle Roo and Auntie Sylv had emerged from the tea tent. They stared up at me, aghast.

I turned to Sancha, who was looking at me with a dumbfounded expression. "Let me," I said. "Please?"

Suddenly self-conscious, she nervously tucked a few matted locks behind her ears. "Thanks," she whispered. Over the mounting fury from the crowd, I could hardly hear her.

"Who's the boy?"

"This auction isn't for children, anyway!"

"Get down from there – where are your parents?"

Snatching the ticket from the presenter, I turned back to face the crowd, trying to set my jaw like Dad did when he wasn't to be messed with.

"This girl is . . . my friend," I said. "Her name is Sancha."

"We don't care what her name is!"

"Get down from there!"

A couple of burly men had started to approach the stage. Just in time, Uncle Roo grabbed one by the arm, while the other just turned and stared, beefy pink palms dropping helplessly to his side.

I swallowed again, the enormity of the moment catching up with me. My stomach flopped like a fish out of water, twisting and turning and gasping for air. I tried to breathe deeply. It was easy to speak if I didn't have to think; if all I had to do was feel something, believe it enough. I couldn't let the silence continue, or else it would overwhelm me completely.

"She's not a Gypsy," I said, hurrying through the words. "She's a Rom. Her people have never owned that land – but they've depended on it for generations. They only want to be able to come back to the place they've always used in the summer. The council – "

"They should try paying tax, like honest people!"

"They're a plague on the villages. They steal! They spread disease!"

"Says who?" I demanded. My head swam with words, dizzying and furious. Yet amid a thousand snatched memories, something from the green book blazed forth in my mind. I inched forward, drawing myself up to withstand the onslaught. "A wise man – a man called Lawrence – said that no one should decide whether other people deserve to be free or not. It's no one's right to decide that."

There were grumbles, but no reply.

"They've been attacked," I continued, voice rising. I could hear myself loud and clear – but it was as if someone else was speaking. "Someone broke a window . . . and scared their horses off. That doesn't sound right to me. It's unfair."

Toward the back of the crowd, a tall, dark figure shifted slowly along the fringes. It was the man with the pipe.

"My father . . ." whispered Sancha.

I turned to the man in the yellow tie and offered him the ticket.

"Well? Will you accept this, or won't you?" I asked. "If they can afford it . . ."

"My father has savings," interrupted Sancha. "In the jar under our bed – and my sister, her dowry . . ."

"Well?"

The little man twitched. "It would have to be authorized by an adult," he whinged.

I looked down into the crowd. Uncle Roo nodded firmly.

"My uncle will authorize it," I said, with a sudden rush of confidence.

"Well . . ." sighed the man, reaching into his suit pocket for something then withdrawing his empty hand. He shuffled his feet, glanced sideways at the crowd, eyed Sancha nervously. "It might be the best way . . . to avoid . . . a confrontation. . . ."

"Three cheers for Dominic!" rose a strong, clear voice from the muddy sea of murmurings. It was Birdie, grinning as giddily as a little kid. Otto joined her, clapping raucously. "Well done, lad!" he bellowed.

I felt someone clasp my hand and saw that Sancha was smiling.

When Lawrence drove into Damascus, hundreds of citizens streamed from their houses to catch a glimpse of the slight Englishman who had raised

the greatest army Arabia had ever seen. A hush
descended as the fair-skinned Prince of Mecca was
proclaimed master of the ancient Arabian capital. At
last, he stopped, and waved – and for miles along
the city roads, the crowds threw up a thrilling
ovation to this strange, young hero.

At that moment, I don't think Lawrence himself
could have been any prouder.

NINETEEN

By now, you'll have guessed who won the baking competition.

"Will Marlo Walker please come forward?" requested the lady in charge of the food stall.

After second and third prizes had gone to a latticed cherry pie and a stunning custard tart topped with glistening blackberries, Marlo's shoulders had begun to slump.

"You've not lost yet," I whispered. And sure enough, she hadn't.

"The committee has selected the pork and apple pies supplied by Miss Walker as this year's Larkspur Baking Champion."

My sister froze, dumbstruck.

"Go on, silly!" I hissed, nudging her forward. "Get up!"

For a moment, I didn't think she would make it. But then, with a deep breath, she rose and picked her way through our row of seats. She looked about three feet taller than usual walking up to accept her prize, blinking as if she had emerged from underground into the glaring light of day for the very first time.

"Why, thank you!" she whispered in disbelief, as the chief sampler – a surprisingly thin woman – gently affixed a blue ribbon to Marlo's collar. A matching ribbon was fastened to the winning pie with a toothpick.

"There was something rather . . . *special* about those pies," said the lady, a look of perplexity crossing her delicate features. Behind her, the tasting committee nodded in unison.

Marlo beamed. "I know exactly what you mean," she said, and the committee of ladies laughed gently, like swans fluttering upon a lake.

"She said they couldn't put their finger on it," gushed Marlo afterwards. "Some thought it was the crust – really biscuity, you know? And then some of the others said no, it's the darkness of the meat because pink would have meant it was cured – and that's bad. And someone *else* thought it was because the sides weren't perfectly straight – it's baked freestanding, so it collapses a little once it's out of the oven. . . ."

She babbled away, tipsy on success. And why shouldn't she be? That tiny blue ribbon had come to mean so much to my little sister that I thought she would explode right then and there. I should have known better. Typically, she cried a little. But I think, for once, it was more to do with happiness than anything else.

Afterwards, Otto clapped me on the back and said, "You'd have done Lawrence proud, Dominic. He was a real champion of lost causes." As a special treat, he took me, Marlo, and Sancha for a ride in his blue MG. Perhaps it wasn't exactly the same as sharing a convoy of armored Rolls Royces with Prince Feisal and the legendary warrior Auda Abu Tayeh, but it came pretty close. I don't think I'd ever felt so brilliant in all my life.

When we arrived at the campsite, I walked with Sancha straight up to her family's wagon. It was the closest I'd ever been to it. From what I could see of the inside, there wasn't much room for four people. Her father crouched on the top step, smoking his pipe. He eyed me very carefully as we approached, and I almost turned back. But Sancha took my hand and led me straight up to him.

"This is Dominic," she said – in English, so I could understand. "He's got us our land."

Nervously, I handed him the certificate that Uncle Roo had signed. I couldn't think of anything to say. Apparently, neither could he. Sancha's father grunted, and folded the paper carefully. Then he looked at Sancha, and jerked his head toward the wagon.

"I'd better go," she said. "See you tomorrow?"

I nodded.

"Thanks, *Nicu*," she said.

Now that Sancha's family was safe, and Marlo had ful-filled her promise to the Reverend, I decided that it was time to fulfill mine.

But when I met Sancha by the quoit the next day, she wasn't smiling.

"What's wrong with you?" I asked.

Sancha was sitting on the capstone, boots trailing several feet above the ground, her wooden leg jutting out stiffly.

"I've got some bad news," she said. Then, pointing to the biscuit tin, "What's in there?"

I opened the tin and unwrapped the terra-cotta fig-urine. "It's a horseman," I said, passing it to her. "Persian, probably. It was given by an Arab lad to an Englishman called T.E. Lawrence, who fought for their freedom. They were great friends."

Sancha was examining the carved figure keenly. "What are you doing with it, then? Isn't it expensive? Why don't you sell it?"

"Apparently little carvings like this one aren't all that rare. It's worth a few shillings, tops. That's what the book says, anyway. Archaeology didn't make Lawrence rich." I closed the tin and set it next to her. "I'd like you to keep it."

"I've always wanted my own horse," smiled Sancha.

"If it weren't for you, I might not have found it at all. If that land had been sold, it could have ended up in the wrong hands . . . it could even have been destroyed. The Reverend wanted me to make sure it would be safe. Will you take care of it, Sancha?"

She nodded.

"What's your news, then?" I asked.

Sancha looked away. Her chin dimpled as she struggled to control a trembling lip. "We're leaving," she said.

"When?"

"Next week."

"But you'll be back, won't you? It's all settled. You can come back whenever you like."

Sancha stared down at me. She sucked at her lip hard and began to swing her leg halfheartedly.

"We're not returning. We're going away — too far to come back."

"But where?" I felt myself flush with panic.

"Europe," she said. "I don't know, exactly. France, maybe. My mother has family there. They've had hard times, too. My father says it's best that we stick together."

"You can't!" I said, rather too loudly. "I stood up for you, Sancha. In front of all those people, we won that land — fair and square!" I kicked wildly at the ground, sending out a spray of skeletal weeds from the black soil. "How could your father turn it down, after all you've been through?"

"It's not his fault!" flared Sancha. She held my gaze, preparing for battle; then appeared to think better of it. "My father is a proud man. They've been planning this for a long time — even before the wagon was attacked.

That was what convinced them. We can't stay here, not after everything that's happened. Even if the land is ours." She stared down at her hands. "It's not fair, I know. But they're grown-ups. They decide."

I slammed my fist to my thigh, willing the pain to overwhelm my anger.

"Why should they decide? They *always* decide. It's just another conspiracy – after all we tried to do. I saved that land for you!"

Sancha spat contemptuously at the ground. "Who says we want to be saved, gadjo? We've always looked after ourselves. We don't need your charity."

Suddenly, my raging felt futile. I clambered up to join her on top of the quoit, and we stared out over the gorse-studded moor for a long time.

"Sancha," I said finally, "What does *Nicu* mean?"

"Eh?" she grunted distractedly.

"*Nicu* – what you said last night."

Sancha smiled wryly. She fixed me with that black gaze, leaning closer.

"It's your name," she whispered.

"What?"

"Every Rom has three names," she explained. "The one their mother gives them when they are born. That name never gets told to anyone else. Then there's the name they use with other Rom. And finally, the name they use for talking to the gadje."

"Is Sancha not your name?" I asked, slightly taken aback. How could you be three people at once?

"It's my gadje name," she explained. "My family calls me Jofranka." She smiled bitterly. "It means 'farmer.' Someone settled; who owns land."

"So, what does Nicu mean?"

"'Victory of the people.'" Sancha elbowed me, trying to be lighthearted. "It's a good name, eh?"

I grinned. Sancha leaned back on her hands, kicking up her bad leg and considering it carefully before continuing. "You can't tell anyone else, though. Only Romany folk. The next time you meet one of my people, you introduce yourself as Nicu, see? Tell them Dominic is just your gadje name."

I nodded.

Sancha gently placed the horseman back in the tin and closed the lid. "I'll keep it safe," she said. "Don't worry."

TWENTY

"You know, Dominic," observed Otto, as we drove to the station on a cool, clear evening, "A certain writer once said that Lawrence had a genius for backing into the limelight." He smiled to himself. "Sounds a bit like someone else I know."

The car was piled with our suitcases once more, and Marlo and I shared the backseat just as we had two months earlier. September was lurking right around the corner, and school would begin in a few weeks. I guess we would have been pretty rotten kids not to want to see our parents again; but it had been hard to say good-bye to Birdie and Auntie Sylv.

"I might be coming up to London sometime soon," Birdie had said. "I'll look you kids up when I'm in town, how's that?"

She had been packing a box with sketchbooks, getting ready to visit a house in Devon that the new tenants were convinced was haunted. As Birdie placed the books between layers of folded canvas, I glimpsed one binding that looked familiar. Reading my curiosity before I even had a chance to speak, Birdie picked up the book and offered it to me with a shrug. "Nothing to see here kiddo," she said. "Just some spooky pictures drawn by a mad old lady, remember?"

Could it be the Reverend's notebook? If it was, then Birdie might have had all the clues she needed to conduct the séance: the whole thing could have been rigged.

I considered the binding more closely. It certainly looked similar to the one I'd seen on the Reverend's desk, but I couldn't be sure that it was exactly the same. Nor did I know for certain that the book I'd seen had been an account of his search for the terra-cotta horseman. For all I knew, it could have been a diary – and in that case, it certainly wasn't mine to read. I already had all the answers I needed, anyway.

"I suppose you're right," I said at last.

For an instant, I could have sworn I detected a flicker of relief in Birdie's eyes.

Marlo sniffed bleakly, clutching the muslin parcel on her lap as we left Zennor behind us. Auntie Sylv had sent us off with enough food to last us fifty train journeys, though I'm not sure that either of us had the stomach for any of it just now.

"It's certainly been an eventful summer," said Uncle Roo with a far-off smile. He twisted around to face us. "Your parents will barely recognize you two. Look at the color on that one!" he grinned, nodding at me. "And Marlo, I expect you'll be cooking up a storm for your old mum just as soon as you set foot in the door."

We'd already been told that Mum was going to need help around the house, even though her cough was gone. The doctor had decided that it wouldn't be necessary to operate on her lungs, but we'd have to wait another few months before she'd be in the clear.

"There aren't any baking competitions where we live," said Marlo. Her ribbon, fixed to one lapel, fluttered in the breeze.

"Well, you'll just have to come back and win the Larkspur prize next year, won't you?" laughed Uncle Roo.

Marlo nodded, allowing herself a small smile.

"Will you be writing to your friend, Dominic?" asked Uncle Roo.

I shook my head, blinking hard as the wind stung my eyes. "She doesn't read very well," I said. "And they don't know where they'll be living. . . ."

"Maybe they'll be back," suggested Otto. "Europe's a hard place for their kind right now. I wouldn't blame them if they turned up here again before too long."

"I hope so," I said. But deep down, I knew it wouldn't happen.

When we arrived at the station, Otto passed me my

suitcase and stuck out his hand. "Put her there," he said, with a brave smile. We shook. Then he patted Marlo on the head. "You take care of your brother," he whispered, reaching for his yellow handkerchief and turning away. Moments later, we heard him blow his nose loudly.

Uncle Roo led us to the platform, where people were already climbing into the train. "I'm proud of you, Dominic," he said. "And your sister."

"Thanks for a lovely time, Uncle Roo," squeaked Marlo, stifling a hiccup.

"It was brilliant," I added, as sturdily as I could.

Our uncle lifted Marlo into the carriage, and passed me the last of the suitcases. "A little gift from the Baron," he said, carefully withdrawing something from his pocket.

It was a white feather. I didn't have a chance to speak before he slammed the door closed and waved to us one last time through the steamed-up window, grinning broadly.

As I leaned back into my seat, I tried to let my mind go blank. The train edged slowly from the station, following the coast for several minutes before veering into green countryside similar to the fields I'd explored with Sancha around Medina Hill.

I tried to imagine Dad's expression when he found out that I could speak. He would slap me on the back and call me a good man – and perhaps he'd start to speak himself. He'd tell me about the war, about Passchendaele. The relief of it might even help Mum get better. We'd be a normal family again.

With one exception, I reminded myself. One word would remain a secret.

Pressing my nose against the window, I watched the condensation from my breath puff across the glass. Plumes of smoke cast racing shadows along the hillside, like specters chasing our train. In the distance, oilseed fields seemed to stretch for miles, the flowers jostling in the breeze like an advancing yellow army.

"Look!"

I sat up, peering out to where Marlo pointed. We were skirting a rugged plateau, train tracks stitching toward the horizon. The expanse reminded me of the desert – the flatness of the land mimicking the flatness of the sea. Through a sparse, barbed screen of trees, glimpses of color flashed in the distance.

They were already on the move.

For several minutes, we traveled alongside the caravan of painted wagons, edging ahead then falling behind as they cut across hidden bends in the land. Briefly, we moved in perfect parallel. But almost as soon as we were exactly aligned, one of their windows directly opposite ours, the wagons began to peel away.

I watched them fade slowly from sight as we rumbled along the tracks that would lead us home.

Acknowledgements

Special thanks to Dr. John Green, Curator of Antiquities at the Ashmolean Museum (Oxford) and to Jonathan Tubb of the British Museum for their advice on arti-facts discovered by Lawrence at Carchemish and Deve Huyuk. The terra-cotta horseman is based on a figurine in the British Museum collection.

Dominic's book is based on *The Boy's Life of Colonel Lawrence* by Lowell Thomas (1927).